Jay Ericson

THOMAS CHRISTOPHER GREENE is the author
of three previous novels. His fiction has been
translated into eleven languages and has won
many awards and honors. In 2007, Tom founded
the Vermont College of Fine Arts, a top fine
arts college, making him the youngest college
president in America at that time. He lives in
Montpelier, Vermont, with his family. Visit him
online at www.thomaschristophergreene.com.

ALSO BY THOMAS CHRISTOPHER GREENE

Envious Moon

I'll Never Be Long Gone

Mirror Lake

Additional Praise for
The Headmaster's Wife

"A layered story of love, unbearable loss, and grief."
—*Fort Worth Star-Telegram*

"[Greene's] prose flows like a thawed stream. . . . Well crafted."
—*The Providence Journal*

"Greene's deft and nimble hand make the story itself a guiltless pleasure to read."
—*The Denver Post*

"What seems to be a deceptively simple story about the headmaster of a New England boarding school and his wife, facing late middle age and growing apart over a difference of opinion about their teenage son, morphed into a haunting, mysterious page-turner. . . . A meditation on longing in all of life's stages, a literary mystery, and a novel with much for book clubs to untangle."
—*Concord Monitor*

"Greene's genre-bending novel of madness and despair evokes both the predatory lasciviousness of Nabokov's classic, *Lolita*, and the anxious ambiguity of Gillian Flynn's contemporary thriller, *Gone Girl*."
—*Booklist*

"Nothing is what it appears in this brilliant story of a life gone awry. . . . The author's true intentions make this tale even more remarkable, for the book is, at its core, a trenchant examination of one family's terrible loss and how the aftermath of tragedy can make or break a person's soul."

—*Publishers Weekly*

"Greene has created a brilliant, harrowing novel depicting the spectacular unraveling of a once distinguished and proudly successful man. He has also conceived one of the most convincingly drawn unreliable narrators that readers may ever meet, a character recalling the creations of Edgar Allan Poe. . . . This is a riveting psychological novel about loss and the terrible mistakes and compromises one can make in love and marriage. Essential for fans of literary fiction." —*Library Journal* (starred review)

"A moving testament to the vicissitudes of love and loss, regret and hope." —*Kirkus Reviews*

"Incredibly beautiful and compulsively readable, *The Headmaster's Wife* will keep you mesmerized into the wee hours. A master storyteller, Greene's biggest achievement is proving that the most complex mystery of all is how and why we love." —Kimberly McCreight, *New York Times* bestselling author of *Reconstructing Amelia*

THE HEADMASTER'S WIFE

Thomas Christopher Greene

Picador

A Thomas Dunne Book
St. Martin's Press
New York

THE HEADMASTER'S WIFE. Copyright © 2014 by Thomas Christopher Greene. All rights reserved. Printed in the United States of America. For information, address Picador, 175 Fifth Avenue, New York, N.Y. 10010.

www.picadorusa.com
www.twitter.com/picadorusa • www.facebook.com/picadorusa
picadorbookroom.tumblr.com

Picador® is a U.S. registered trademark and is used by St. Martin's Press under license from Pan Books Limited.

For book club information, please visit www.facebook.com/picadorbookclub or e-mail marketing@picadorusa.com.

The Library of Congress has cataloged the St. Martin's Press edition as follows:

Greene, Thomas Christopher, 1968–
    The headmaster's wife / Thomas Christopher Greene.—1st ed.
        p. cm.
    ISBN 978-1-250-03894-4 (hardcover)
    ISBN 978-1-4668-3424-8 (e-book)
    1. School principals—Fiction. 2. Boarding schools—Fiction. 3. Psychic trauma—Fiction. 4. Grief—Fiction. 5. Marriage—Fiction. I. Title.
    PS3607.R453 H43 2014
    813'.6—dc23

                                                              2013031656

Picador Paperback ISBN 978-1-250-06233-8

Picador books may be purchased for educational, business, or promotional use. For information on bulk purchases, please contact the Macmillan Corporate and Premium Sales Department at 1-800-221-7945, extension 5442, or write to specialmarkets @macmillan.com.

First published in the United States by Thomas Dunne Books, an imprint of St. Martin's Press

First Picador Edition: March 2015

D 10 9 8 7 6 5 4

For Jane

ACRIMONY

He arrives at the park by walking down Central Park West and then entering through the opening at West Seventy-seventh Street. This is in the winter. It is early morning, and the sun is little more than an orangey haze behind heavy clouds in the east. Light snow flurries fill the air. There are not many people out, a few runners and women bundled against the cold pushing strollers.

He walks down the asphalt drive and when he reaches a path with a small wooden footbridge he stops for a moment, and it is there somewhere, a snatch of memory, but he cannot reach it. An elderly couple comes toward him, out for their morning walk. The man gives him a hearty good morning but he looks right through him. What is it he remembers? It is something beautiful, he is sure of it, but it eludes him like so many things seem to do nowadays.

If he could access it, what he would see was a day twenty years earlier, in this same spot. Though it was not winter, but a bright fall day, the maples bleeding red, and he is not alone. Elizabeth is here, as is his son, Ethan. They had gone to the museum and then had lunch before coming into the park. Ethan's first trip to New York, and he is five, and though he loved the museum with its giant dinosaur skeletons, it is the park that draws his attention. The day could not be more glorious. Seasonably warm and without a cloud in the sky: a magical Manhattan day.

Ethan runs ahead of them on the path. His wife takes his arm, leans into him. He looks down and smiles at her. They don't need to speak, for they are both drinking in the moment, the day, the happiness of their boy, and the gift of this experience. There is no reason to give it words.

Ethan finds a gnarled tree on the side of the path, one that grows horizontally just a foot or so above the ground. He immediately climbs up on top of it, shimmying his little body over its trunk, and the two of them sit on a bench a few feet away and watch him.

A couple of times they suggest they should keep walking, but the boy will not have it. He has found a tree perfectly suited for him and he demands in the way that children do that he be watched, admired, and studied as he climbs it one way, then the other. And this is okay, for they are in no rush. It is a small moment, but a perfect one. The child is right: Where else would they rather be? What could be more complete?

Now, standing on the same path, with the snow picking up and falling more steadily around him, he gives up trying to find this memory and instead focuses on the snow, tracing individual flakes as they come in front of his field of vision and then disappear. He is alone suddenly. There is no one walking in either direction. The park is his. He takes off his hat and places it on the ground. Then he removes his jacket. Next he undoes his tie and then his shirt and his undershirt. Soon he is naked, and he sets off again, leaving his clothes in a neat pile on the path, and he moves up and over the hilly terrain, his eyes straight ahead, oblivious to the people who gasp when they come around a corner to find him marching toward them. All that matters to him is the feel of his bare feet crunching wonderfully on the crusty snow beneath him.

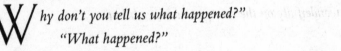

"Why don't you tell us what happened?"

"What happened?"

"Yes."

"Where should I start?"

"Where do you want to start?"

He looks at the men sitting across from him. It is a stupid question, he thinks.

He says, "At the beginning, of course."

"That would be helpful," says the man who does all the talking.

"Why do you care?"

"What do you mean?"

"I mean, why do you care? Just as it sounds." He was growing exasperated. "What am I to you?"

"Sir, do we need to refresh you on how we found you?"

"I was in the park."

One of the men laughs. The other one silences him with his hand. *"Yes, you were in the park. Naked. Twenty-degree weather. Snow on the ground. Walking in Central Park naked."*

"Is that a crime?"

"Yes. It is, in fact."

"In Vermont it's not."

"Seriously?"

"Yes. You can be naked. You just can't be obscene."

"What's the difference?"

He sighs. He looks down at his clothes. They are too big for him. He is practically swimming in these damn clothes.

"Do I have to answer that?"

"No."

"Good. Because that will tire me."

"Just start, then."

"Okay," he says. *"But I want some coffee. Strong coffee. Black."*

The man nods. *"We'll get that for you. Begin."*

He leans forward. *"The beginning,"* he says. *"This is how it starts."*

7

It starts with the most innocent of gestures. She does something girls the world over do. She uses her long fingers to pull strands of straw-colored hair behind her ears.

She is leaning over her book at her desk in the front row. I have not noticed her before, though it is only the second day since I've returned to the classroom. She is rather unremarkable. Maybe I've passed her on the walks around campus, but I don't remember seeing her before.

She looks up. She is pretty but in a sad-eyed Slavic kind of way. Her face slightly off-center, green eyes with small bags under them that will only grow with age, her skin clear and pink. I get lost looking at her. I forget for a moment the rest of the class, and when she turns her gaze away from the blackboard behind me to my face, I become aware of all the eyes on me. Time to speak. I look over their heads and find my voice.

It was the chair of the board's idea that I step back into the classroom. At first the suggestion angered me. Especially how it was framed. You seem distracted, Arthur, Dick Ives said to me after the last board meeting.

"Just didn't bring my A game, Dick," I said.

"It's not just that," said Dick. "More of a general feeling the board has."

"This isn't about golf again, is it?" It is well known that I hate golf. It is a silly game. Hitting a tiny ball with a stick for hours on end, and the board has been after me to do more of it. That donors expect it. For the life of me I have never been able to figure out what golf has to do with education at the Lancaster School.

"God, no," Dick said. "It might benefit you to get back to your first love. Dip your toe in. Get closer to the mission. The capital campaign is done. Couldn't be a better time."

And so in the fall I return to my old discipline, English, by teaching one class. I choose the Russians. I always loved the Russians—Pushkin and Lermontov; Gogol, Turgenev, and Chekhov; Dostoevsky and the great Tolstoy. The atmosphere, the ethos of their work. They remind me of Vermont in November. Dark moors and muted colors, landscapes awash in brown. Lives determined by birth-right and accidents of fate.

Anyway, immediately I see the wisdom of Dick's advice. Standing in the classroom with the fall sun streaming through the windows, looking out over my charges, hearing the rise and fall of my voice—it is like I am transported back in time. I am twenty-four again, a year removed from Yale. In the classroom, where I belong. Literature matters. Literature is important. This, I think, is why you raise money, why you build buildings, why you endure endless bus travel over these hills for Wednesday and Saturday sporting events. Because in few corners of the world can you find the deeper human truths still being taught as they should be. The kind of truths that mold minds and create leaders. Lancaster has yet to produce a president, though it has come close. Perhaps in this room in front of me, I imagine, sits one of them.

I turn my attention back to the classroom. Handsome, preppy teenagers, the lot of them. The chosen ones. I pose a question, and it pleases me. The way it is constructed, grand enough to be rhetorical but also grounded.

I look around. A few hands go up. I look over at her. Her hand is raised. She looks confident. Something about her speaks to me, and I cannot figure out what. I call on her and I don't fully hear what she says, though she has a nice voice. Instead I am fixated on her face, as if somewhere in those sad eyes resides a clue as to why her pulling her hair behind her ears has made me notice her in a way that tells me that it has been a long time since I have noticed anything at all.

THE HEADMASTER'S WIFE

T hat night at dinner I look for her. My table, the headmaster's table, is at the far end of the great dining room with its high ceilings and chandeliers. My own chair always faces the entirety of the room, the great arched windows behind me. Every three weeks the students rotate tables. The idea is that, in time, they get to know the entire faculty and their families. It is a good system, I guess, though sometimes I wish we could follow other schools and move away from formal dining. My father would disagree, but I never liked the small talk.

I look over at my wife, Elizabeth. She has decided to come to dinner tonight. She does not appear all the time anymore, which is unusual for a spouse at Lancaster, especially for the wife of the head of school. Elizabeth is wearing tennis clothes. I frown. Hardly appropriate. Tennis is her new and overwhelming obsession these past years. She plays as soon as her work at the library ends, and often rises before I do to hit serve after serve from a raised bucket on one of the indoor courts. This I cannot understand, though she tells me she finds it hypnotic and therapeutic.

"Just serving over and over to no one?" I say to her once.

"Yes," she says.

"I don't get it."

"There are lots of things you don't get about me," she says.

As I am remembering this, one of the students at the table, a redheaded sophomore boy who fancies himself a clown, is telling a story. He is from a well-known family, and this adolescent clownishness I have seen dozens of times. It is his way of drawing attention to himself, and while not particularly endearing to adults now, it will serve him well later. I half-listen to his story, something about Mr. Linder's math class, though the other kids laugh heartily, as does Elizabeth.

And then I see her. She comes out of the kitchen with a tray in her hand. She is waiting tables, which isn't what it sounds like, since all the students at Lancaster are required to have campus jobs. Though any jobs associated with the cafeteria are among the least desirable, and at the minimum she is not a star athlete. All the athletes get simple jobs, like cleaning the basketball courts, which is done by the maintenance crew anyway.

I turn to Elizabeth and whisper, "This girl, coming by with the tray, do you know her?"

Elizabeth looks up. "She's new. Why?"

"She's in my class. Said something interesting, that's all."

"Jewish," says Elizabeth softly.

"Interesting."

"What's interesting about that?"

"Nothing," I say, though a picture begins to form in my mind. She is new and a junior, which is rare at Lancaster, and suggests she is smart. An overachiever from a suburban high school, Westchester perhaps, or even New Jersey, Short Hills or some such place. New-money parents. Dad an ambulance-chasing attorney or in middle management at Morgan Stanley. Commutes into the city. Mom who favors yellow gold, lots of it.

She walks by our table. The tray is full of ramekins of Jell-O, heading for a nearby table. I contemplate the shape of her beneath her clothes. She is full breasted but otherwise unremarkable. This is her peak, I think rather ungenerously. She will never be this beautiful again.

The headmaster's house is a white Colonial that sits on the main road that runs through the quiet town of Lancaster, Vermont. Behind it are soccer fields and dorms, and beyond those runs the Connecticut River, slow and fat. The house is large and designed for entertaining, with tall, high-ceilinged rooms downstairs. The upstairs originally had four bedrooms, though it now has only three, as my father, when he was head of school, turned one of them into an office, which I still use.

After dinner Elizabeth and I go upstairs. It is early, but as is our pattern now, she stops at the top of the stairs and gives me her cheek. I lay a soft kiss on it. She goes to our bedroom, which has become her room exclusively. I sleep in the guest room. It was never anything we talked about,

15

and I do not remember precisely when it first started. But we are happier this way. Married people often forget how nice it is to sleep alone.

The other bedroom was once mine, when I was a child, and later belonged to our son, Ethan. It is still Ethan's room, I suppose, and Elizabeth has refused to take down any of his things. His clothes still hang in the closet, his athletic trophies are still on the bureau. Ethan wanted out of Lancaster. After graduation he spurned Yale (and by so doing, spurned me) and became a soldier. He went to Iraq, and Elizabeth does nothing but worry about him. He disappoints me. Not that there is anything wrong with serving one's country. And despite what you may think, I do not need him to return here as I did, or as my father and grandfather did. I do not need him to, though it surprises me that he chose to impetuously close the door to that possibility. Though that is another story.

As is my habit, I go into my study. I pour several fingers of scotch from the fifth I keep in the bottom right drawer of the large wooden desk. I nurse the scotch and absentmindedly turn on the laptop and review the day's e-mail. But something has me restless.

I drain the scotch and go downstairs to fetch my coat.

Outside, the fall air is cool but the night is clear and without moon. Full of stars. I like to walk at night. It is mandatory study hall time, and all the students are in their rooms or, with special permission, at the library.

Normally I head for the heart of campus, crossing the street and into the quadrangle, with its historic granite academic buildings and upper-class boys' dorms. I like having this part of the campus to myself. Alone with the history of it all. But tonight I walk the other way, out across the soccer fields. The grass dewy on my shoes.

I walk toward the four squat brick buildings that were built in the late 1960s to accommodate the new type of Lancaster student: girls. I was a freshman the year Lancaster went co-ed. My father made the decision with the board, and it was controversial at the time, especially with alumni, though also with my classmates. I am still not sure what we feared would be lost.

The buildings themselves I have always found an eyesore. Out of character with the rest of the campus, which is a tasteful mixture of stately granite and early-nineteenth-century clapboard homes, they are brick and featureless and were built on the cheap. When I was a student we called them the projects, though it has been a long time since I have heard that particular terminology. Then again, as headmaster, you hear less and less.

I come down the small slope from the soccer field and then cross the pavement that separates the dorms and the field. The four buildings are in front of me, close together, separated by narrow alleys of grass. Each building is two stories, and the first-floor windows are close enough to the ground that years ago we put in place what we call the "one-foot rule." Boys visiting from the upper campus must have at least one foot on the ground at all times when visiting the windows, which they do most evenings.

I walk between the first two buildings, Fuller and Jameson Halls. The windows are lit up, and the shades are all open. Inside are girls at their desks, girls lying facedown on their beds with books in front of them. Their doors open to the hallways inside, as they are required to do. I pause in front of each window and look in, and while part of me knows there is something entirely untoward about the headmaster staring into the windows of the upper-class girls' dorms, I am unfazed by it tonight. Not a single girl as much as looks up. I am an apparition.

I make it through the first set of dorms, and then the second alleyway. It is on the third and final pass that I finally see her. Hers is a corner room, with two windows, one that faces the alley and another that looks toward the river.

She is at the desk closest to the alley window. Beyond her is her roommate, a girl I recognize, Meredith something or other, from New York. Her father is a prominent attorney specializing in mergers and acquisitions. Someone the board has targeted for cultivation.

We are separated only by glass. She is reading for my

class: Lermontov's *A Hero of Our Time*. Reading that is not even due for a week. She is ahead, which says something about her. She wears sweatpants and one of those tight white tank tops that all the girls seem to wear these days. The ones that don't even attempt to cover their bellies. As if sensing me, she suddenly looks up and then toward the window. I quickly step back.

She has not seen me. She stands and arches her back like a cat. Her breasts are indeed full beneath the tank top, and her belly has only the slightest of outward curves.

What is this? I am the headmaster of the elite Lancaster School. I have been around young women my whole life and have never so much as given their bodies more than passing consideration. That part of my mind has been closed for a long time. And now here I find myself, on a cool fall night under the stars on the old campus that has been my home for fifty-three of my fifty-seven years, peering through a window at an eighteen-year-old girl.

19

The following Monday I announce to my class that I will be providing office hours to any student who would like to discuss the assigned reading or who might have questions about the first paper I have asked them to write. I expect to see her. Her earnestness suggests she is the type to take advantage of office hours. I am getting a sense of her: She is grateful to be at Lancaster. Many take it for granted. She is not one of them.

In the meantime, I've discovered what I can about her. She is different from what I thought. First, her name is Betsy Pappas. The name sounds Greek, not Jewish, but you can never be sure. She is not from New Jersey at all, but instead from Vermont, the small Northeast Kingdom town of Craftsbury. She is a scholarship student. She tested off the charts at some tiny Podunk school and is on a full ride. The family has no money to speak of. Her father teaches woodshop at a small college up there. What a thing to teach at a college. Last I checked, carpenters didn't require a college education.

Her mother makes jewelry. There is one sibling, a younger sister who still attends the Podunk school. Betsy has redone her junior year, which is a requirement at Lancaster. Transfers have to spend at least two years to get their degree. She turned eighteen in August.

It's an entirely different portrait from the one I imagined. Instead of new-money suburban Jews, they are no-money Vermont hippies. I picture an aging, run-down farmhouse, a pickup truck and a VW van in the driveway.

With that bit of research settled, my workweek proceeds on in typical fashion. Mrs. LaForge, who has been the headmaster's secretary for close to forty years, keeps the schedule moving. Meetings come in half-hour increments, and there are set-aside times for me to make calls to the heavy hitters who keep the wheels of Lancaster greased. In between, I deal with discipline cases. This week there is a sophomore boy who was found to have an ounce of marijuana in a cigar box hidden in his bureau during a room inspection. Drug cases are normally a swift exit from the school, but as with all things, there are nuances at play. The boy is a Mellon, of the Pennsylvania Mellons, and the boy, an arrogant, chubby kid with a mop of brown hair, knows this makes an easy decision complicated. The boy shows no fear in the headmaster's office. He sits comfortably, sunk back in one of the leather chairs like he doesn't have a care in the world.

When I was younger, I might have just gone by the book, but with age you come to terms with the fact that not everyone arrives into this world on an equal footing. There is no real equity at boarding school. There are the Mellons, and then there are the Betsy Pappases from Craftsbury, Vermont. Justice is not blind at Lancaster. I call the boy's father and let him know I will make an exception to the normal policy, but that if it happens again I will not be able to be so generous. The father says he understands and will have a difficult talk with Junior. It goes without saying that a check will arrive in the coming week. History says it will be significant.

On Wednesday, Deerfield, one of our fiercest rivals, comes to campus, and I spend the afternoon touring the sporting events. Mrs. LaForge maps them out for me on my phone, one of the many clever things she does to make me look good, and a beep goes off when I am supposed to move to the next event. A quarter of the football game, off to boys' soccer for fifteen minutes, then to girls' soccer, and finally to the finish line of the cross-country race. A light rain falls on a dull gray day, and not many parents make the trip. Nevertheless I do my best to summon the slick enthusiasm my role as chief booster demands, moving up the sidelines under my umbrella, shaking hands, talking to parents about their children, patting faculty on the back.

Everyone is happy to see me, or pretends to be. Whatever they think of me personally, they respect the office. That is one thing I have learned. Like it or not, I am the face of Lancaster, and they are suitably pleased that I have graced their particular game with my presence, which is entirely the point.

On Friday, I hop a flight from Lebanon, New Hampshire, to Manhattan, and that evening, at the Lancaster Club, I move among the well-heeled alumni who have come out to hear me speak. In the large wood-paneled room with its deep-set leather furniture, I rise to speak, glass of wine in hand, and for a moment the old doubt comes over me. I have been doing this a long time, you see, but sometimes I still feel like a fraud. I do not know if I really ever wanted to be head of school. I am not my father, as my son is not I. The older alums still compare me to my father, and I know they find me wanting. I am not starchy enough, perhaps, a pale imitation of the old man's greatness. I do not have his stentorian voice. But tonight I do a reasonable job of bringing forth that old love of school. I give my stump speech. I tell them about the cantilevered glass addition to the library, the new tech center, the field house under construction that will be the envy of all the great New England schools. I have facts at the tip of my tongue: the percentage of graduates who will go on to Ivies next year (53 percent, best among the competition), the accomplishments of faculty, and of course all the news on the beloved sports teams.

I wear my Lancaster tie, black and gold with small crests on it, and for a moment it is as if nothing has changed. I am doing what I have always done, what you could say I was born to do. The old school has given me my life.

Mrs. LaForge brings her into my office and then closes the door on her way out. The girl sits in one of the tall wingback chairs in front of my desk. I take in her clothes and see she is in full compliance of the dress code. White blouse buttoned appropriately, knee-length skirt, close-toed shoes fully laced. On her lap are three of the novels from my class.

"Betsy," I say, saying her name for the first time, feeling it in my mouth.

She looks up at me expectantly. "Yes?"

"You are enjoying the Russians?"

"I like the realists."

I nod. "Which of the books we have read speaks to you the most?"

"Turgenev. It seems . . . relevant."

"Expand on that, please."

"His view of love. Of marriage. He seems to be constantly questioning the importance of institutions while reaffirming them at the same time. And the struggle of the two brothers to find their place in the world seems similar to my own experience."

I smile. "Are you struggling to find your place in the world?"

"We all are," Betsy says.

She shifts in her chair now and crosses her legs. There is the sense of white flesh beneath her skirt.

"Surely the struggle is different now than in nineteenth-century Russia."

"I don't know about that. The trappings are different. Technology and so on. Ways of travel. But those are all surface things. The elemental truths are the same."

"The elemental truths?" I lean back in my chair and stroke my chin thoughtfully.

"Love and family. Fathers and sons. Mothers and daughters."

"What about economics?"

"Like serfdom?"

"Yes."

"It still exists, just under different names."

"Are we a young Marxist, Ms. Pappas?"

"No. It's just that the idea of America as a meritocracy is an illusion designed to make the elite feel better."

"Designed?" I say. "That implies someone is calling the shots."

"It's self-perpetuating," she says.

"What about a black president who was born poor and raised by his grandmother in a Hawaii apartment? Doesn't that refute your premise?"

"Not at all," Betsy says. "To maintain the illusion, a few have to be allowed through. Anyway, the presidency isn't a good example."

This makes me laugh. "The presidency? The leader of the free world?"

She shrugs. "Presidents still work for others."

I look beyond her to the wide windows that line my office. On the quad the large maples have turned the brightest of red, their leaves catching the afternoon sun and lifting their color as if they are on fire.

"I have an idea," I say. "Next week I have to go to an alumni gathering in Boston. I would like you to come."

"Me?"

"I sometimes bring promising students. So the alumni can meet the new generation of Lancaster students. And see the minds their scholarship gifts support."

She smiles. She likes this. A proud phone call back to the parents. She looks down for a moment. When she looks back up, her hair falls in front of her face, and she does that thing again, pulling the blond strands behind her ears.

"Okay, then," I say. "Mrs. LaForge will make the arrangements with your dorm parent and see you are forgiven your classes that day."

"Thank you, Mr. Winthrop," Betsy says, as if sensing her time has come to an end.

"You're welcome, Betsy," I say.

It is not at all calculated, this idea of bringing her to Boston. The amazing thing is that it comes to me on the spur of the moment. Now, it is true I have brought students to alumni gatherings before, but mostly a star quarterback and the like, some prize horse to show off to the donors. I have never brought someone undistinguished in the obvious ways. Betsy is a very bright scholarship student, and the alumni will certainly be happy to meet a young woman who is a prime example of the importance of these kinds of contributions. Opening the world of Lancaster to the gifted, regardless of progeny. Nevertheless, I am concerned that her charms are below the surface, you see—a subtle but agile mind and a beauty that is invisible to the rest of the world.

I do not feel the least bit awkward about letting others know she is coming. One of the advantages of being head of school is that, in matters like this, others will assume only purity of motive. And while it crosses my mind— one can never be too careful when it comes to female students—it is hard to imagine anyone suspecting an attraction on my part. What is it I would see in Betsy Pappas? If I were truly to be interested in a female student, it would hardly be this unremarkable daughter of hippies from the woods, now, would it?

"A gifted student," I tell Mrs. LaForge once Betsy has left. "Surprising. Interesting ideas on literature." I continue, pacing in the outer office, moving to the window and then back to her desk. "Yes, very interesting, Mrs. LaForge. You do not come across young women like that very often."

Mrs. LaForge watches me from the pile of paperwork on her large desk. She does not say anything, which is par for the course with Mrs. LaForge. She assumes all my statements are rhetorical unless I am very direct.

The notion of the pending trip lifts my spirits. In the days preceding it there is a noticeable spring in my step. I bound out of bed to get my morning coffee before heading across the street to the dining hall. I cheerily greet all I pass on the campus walkways. Talking to me on the phone, Dick Ives appears to notice something in my voice.

"You sound good, Arthur," he says.

"Brilliant idea about the classroom, Dick," I say.

"You are enjoying it, then? Perfect."

I don't mind the September rain that falls ceaselessly, day after day, dulling the seasonal color. And even Elizabeth, interrupting my post-dinner scotch in my office wanting to talk, cannot jar me out of this feeling. Something is happening, I know it. Even the presence of Elizabeth, once-beautiful Elizabeth, now with her gray hair cut short across her forehead like a man's, cannot knock me out of it.

But first I must listen to my wife. I try to be patient, though it is a conversation we have had before, and I do not invite her to sit. She stands in front of my desk. For a while now we have been moving around this old house like a pair of ghosts. Sometimes I feel like I live alone.

"You have to deal with this, Arthur," Elizabeth says. "You cannot just ignore it."

"I am not ignoring anything," I say calmly. "I just don't see any reason why I need to dwell on all this, which is what you are asking me to do."

"You have to come to terms with it," she says. "You cannot hide from this."

"Is this about Ethan again?"

"No, this is about me. It's like you . . . forget it. It's no use."

I raise my hand to stop her. "Elizabeth," I say. "I know full well what happened. I know all of it."

"How come you won't talk about it? It's not normal."

"What is normal?" I say. "No one can answer that, can they? I am dealing with this in my own way. As are you."

I look down at my desk now. There are some papers there, a draft strategic plan the academic dean put together that I really need to look at. I pick it up absentmindedly and am instantly fixated on the first paragraph (a spelling mistake of all things), so that I do not even hear Elizabeth until she is on top of me, pushing my chest and crying.

"Elizabeth, for Christ's sake," I say.

"Fucking wake up, Arthur," she says. "I know someone is still in there."

"Okay," I say. "Calm down, please. Calm down."

Her body goes slack in my arms, though she feels oddly weightless. I take her in my arms. Her body heaves with heavy, racking sobs. I know what to do. I run one hand through her hair and then pull back and look at her, at her gray eyes, at the pronounced crow's feet that fan out from their corners.

She dresses for the occasion, more than the normal school requirements of safe preppiness. She wears beige heels, a black dress, and a small cardigan sweater she holds tightly around her breasts as she steps into the passenger side of my Saab. There is something different about her, and it takes me a moment to realize what it is. It is makeup. She wears lipstick and eye shadow. There is something cheap about it, like a child playing dress-up, and for an instant after she is in the car, I am disappointed in her. And in this disappointment I also find relief, for now I can just take her to Boston and back to school and forget about her.

But then we are on the road. I like to drive. I love that sense of mastery you get from country roads, where the road rises and falls and the fields stretch out to the river and you bend the car around sharp curves, and where just when you think you are going to lose control, the machine corrects itself and brings you back into line. If only life could be so simple.

We talk casually. She tells me about her family. I ask her all the right questions. I draw her out. I have experience in this, generations of reticent students and donors. Betsy does not need my help of course, for she is at ease with herself. Far beyond her years. I even forget the makeup that bothered me, and as we drive, I focus on the soft lilt of her voice, her stories, and it is like the years between us somehow disappear and we are just two adults traveling on a weekend trip. To the Cape, perhaps, or up to Maine. Some B and B where we will eat dinner and retire to a tasteful room to become lovers.

At dusk we cross the Zakim Bridge, shiplike with lights strung across its high curved beams. Soon we are in the city. I watch her next to me. She looks up at the buildings as we drive through the Back Bay, past the brownstones and down streets full of people. She has known only the Vermont woods and, to her, Boston must seem like another world.

The alumni event is at the top of the Prudential Center. I have never liked heights, but Betsy has the fearlessness of youth. From the great windows she looks out into the twinkling fall night, her fingers stretched out across the panes of glass. Across the harbor to the ocean in the distance. Airplanes swooping in from the sea. The buildings of the Financial District rising up like a bulwark against the water.

I bring her around and introduce her to those I know, and to others I introduce myself, though no introduction is necessary. Everyone who has come knows who I am.

Betsy comports herself well. She makes eye contact. She talks about what she loves about Lancaster. She says all the right things. She even has kind words for my class. She tells a ruddy-faced member of the class of '54 that the Russians teach you how to live today. I am touched by this, naturally, and I could not agree more.

There are two rules to alumni gatherings that are unspoken but understood in my line of work. The first is that you take it easy on the wine. The second is that you are never photographed with a drink in your hand. The second I follow this time by handing off my wine to Betsy, who is always there, like an eager assistant. I cannot help but imagine her drinking the ruby wine, see it staining her lips.

The first dictum (take it easy on the wine), I ignore this night. I drink far too much, and by the time things are winding down, I am not nearly as together as I should be.

As we ride the elevator down and then walk out onto the street, it is apparent to me that I am in no condition to drive. Lancaster is three hours away, and it is already nine o'clock at night. I do not say any of this to my young charge, of course. Instead I say to her, "Do you mind walking for a little bit? I like to stretch my legs before getting back into the car."

If this confuses her, she says nothing. We begin to walk. It is a lovely night in Boston, with only the slightest of fall bites to the mild breeze. It is early, and the streets are full of people. I am tempted to offer her my arm, but it is a terribly old-fashioned thing to do.

Soon we make our way across the Common and through the wide avenues of the Back Bay. We do not talk, and Betsy seems smitten with the night. I watch as she takes it all in; the people, the homeless men on the benches, the glassy rise of the John Hancock, improbably tall next to buildings and churches from another time.

On Newbury Street we stroll past restaurants and stores. Immaculate brownstones. We are aimless, the two of us, and feeling the wine in my head, I know I should say something, that I am the leader here, but I cannot do it. We just walk and walk. At one point I am looking over at her, and she is gazing across the street at diners spilling out of a basement-level French restaurant. Fashionable people not much older than Betsy. A wry, knowing smile comes across her face, and when she turns back to meet my gaze, I am overcome.

I pull her toward me, awkwardly. It is so clumsy, this embrace, unannounced, and I have a sudden moment of clarity, that I am about to do something that will change my life forever. Something that will undo in a second all I have done. Nevertheless, she is in my arms, and against a waist-high wrought-iron fence, I kiss her forcefully on the mouth.

I am prepared to blame it on drunkenness. Another small blight of erratic behavior in a year of behaving oddly. I am prepared to be slapped. I am prepared to be repelled.

But Betsy Pappas does not recoil from me in the shadows of Newbury Street. She kisses me back. If anything, she is more passionate than I am. My hands are in her hair, at the back of her head. Our lips come together. Our teeth clash for a moment as we search for each other's open mouths. Her tongue hot against my teeth. Warm breath intermingling. I run my hand along her back, and she moves into me.

A few passersby come within feet of us, but this is the city and they do not pay us any attention. Her back is to them, and there is something amazingly normal and romantic about two lovers kissing on a fall night. As for me, I am oblivious to all except what is in front of me, the firmness of my hand on her back, her mouth on mine, her smell, clean as baby powder.

It is an ancient lust that roils inside me. We make our way back toward the Common, and every ten feet or so, it seems, we stop in the shadows and fall once again in each other's embrace. At one point I say in a hushed tone, "We can't do this."

"We can," she says back, and they are the words I want to hear.

I am crazy with lust. My heart beats like a sparrow in a hand. We move quickly across the Common and to the great granite façade of the Copley Hotel. Doormen whisk us into the stately lobby with its friezes and marble and ceiling painted a pale Michelangelo blue. At the counter we are a May–December romance, a sudden change of plans, no luggage. A place for the night, if you please.

Upstairs, Betsy ducks into the bathroom while I make a quick phone call to school. I am practically incoherent on the phone. I reach her dorm parent, a Mr. Crane. It is right before lights-out. In the background I hear girls scurrying. "Yes, of course, Mr. Winthrop," he says, when I plead car trouble and say I will be finding a place for Betsy Pappas to stay for the night in Boston. He does not ask where, and I do not tell him.

I dim the lights. Betsy comes to me. I undress her from where I sit on the edge of the bed. She is magnificent. She turns her head away from me, toward the window that looks out on the Common, the orangeish light of the city and the sounds of traffic. I nuzzle my face in her belly. Her inexperienced skin is soft and pliant. She moans softly. She is greedy to know, though I believe this is not her first time. Some kid pushing into her inside a car in Northern Vermont. I try not to think of this, but instead am torn between the exclusive feelings of deep tenderness and a desire to own her.

I remind myself to be slow. This is not the furied and practiced act of the long married. I need to discover her. I want her to discover me.

Afterward, we lie spent on the bed. This is the hard part. The lust has left me, like air expelled from a balloon. Her head rests contentedly on my chest. I absentmindedly play with her hair. Outside, a siren wails, a sudden and harsh reminder of the rest of the world.

I reach for the phone and order a bottle of wine to be sent to the room. I felt better earlier, when my blood was full of alcohol.

I am the first to speak. I say, "You can't fall in love with me."

She surprises me by laughing. She rises off the bed and walks toward the window. I watch her full buttocks as she walks. "You have nothing to worry about from me," she says.

"No?" I say. It dawns on me that the language of love, the very word, *love,* may not be the lingua franca of her generation. Maybe no one talks about love anymore, maybe there is some other language I am not privy to. Everything grows coarser over time, less subtle. There is no mysticism anymore. Perhaps love is too high-minded.

Betsy cracks open the window, and the night air comes in, along with all the sounds of the cars passing by the Common, the stop-and-start, the diesel roar of a bus. "You have nothing to worry about from me," she says again.

"Good," I say, though secretly this dismays me. Right now I want things from her to worry about.

She goes to her pocketbook and, to my great surprise, pulls out a pack of cigarettes.

"You smoke?" I say incredulously, and the boundaries between us return for a moment, as I am the headmaster and she is the student.

She laughs again. "Sometimes," she says. So mature, I think. Look at her. She pads across the room to the window again and lights her cigarette, exhales into the night.

"These are all No Smoking rooms," I say.

She looks back at me. She impresses again. "Are we suddenly obeying the rules?"

I feel old and silly. I look down at my hairy chest, my

slight gut—not bad for a man of my age—and then to my tired cock. "No," I say. "No rules tonight."

Betsy leans out the window. Her ass is in the air, and I feel a stirring again. She turns back toward me. She says, "I just wanted to check the box, you know."

"Check the box?"

"The one next to 'older man.'"

I realize I have underestimated her again. The knock comes to the door, and she drops her cigarette out the window and hustles to the bathroom. Closes the door behind her. I rise and put on a terrycloth robe, and Room Service brings in a bottle of wine in a bucket. The man asks me if he should open it. I nod. He does. There are two glasses. I can see him taking in the smell of smoke and the lower-note, but still undeniable, smell of our sex. I sign, and he leaves.

I pour two glasses of wine. Betsy returns from the bathroom, the closing door apparently her cue. A towel is wrapped around her. All sense of propriety has gone out the window, and I hand her a glass of wine. She takes it from me and drinks.

I look at the clock. It reads ten past eleven. At home I would be in bed now, reading, and it would be past lights-out for Betsy. As if reading my mind, she says, "It's early."

She jumps onto the bed. I join her. There is nothing to say. I turn on the television, and we sit together drinking wine and watching a movie on HBO. I pay no attention to it. She lies next to me, and the towel falls from her breasts, the rich ripeness of her youth spilling out onto the sheets. Later we make love again, and this time it is different, the lights off, and I am filled with a deep urgency. She is on all fours, and I look over her to the windows and the refracted light of the city. I hold her shoulders in my hands and feel the bones moving quietly underneath her skin.

H e stops talking as another man comes into the room. The man is African-American and tall and leans down toward the man who does all the talking and whispers something inaudible in his ear. The man who does all the talking nods, and then the African-American man backs out of the room.

"Do you want me to stop?"

"No, continue. Unless you want a break. You can have one, you know."

"What was that about?"

"What?"

"The man who came in. What did he tell you?"

"He confirmed your identity."

"My identity?"

"That an Arthur Winthrop who fits your general description was the headmaster at the Lancaster School in Vermont."

"Was that in doubt?"

"Routine," the man says. "We have to check these things out. You understand."

"One part you have wrong. You said *was* the headmaster. I am *the* headmaster."

"Of course. Just a figure of speech."

"Not a figure of speech. It was the wrong tense."

"My apologies," the man says, and he smiles. "Forgive me. And please, continue."

"Can I have more coffee?"

"Sure."

"And a cigarette?"

"I didn't know you smoked."

"Sometimes I do."

"It's a public building, but if you don't tell anyone, I think we can make an exception."

The man who doesn't talk gets up and leaves the room. "Should I wait for him to come back?"

"No, you can continue. He'll get your coffee and a smoke."

"Thank you."

The next morning, under steely skies, I drop her off at the front of her dorm and return home and take a long hot shower before making way across the road to my office. The campus feels different to me somehow. I can't pinpoint why, but it feels smaller maybe, the buildings closing in on themselves. It is more than the usual feeling I get when I return from Boston or New York. Something has changed, but I do not know what.

It is only later, when I am back in the swing of my work—meetings and phone calls and the things one does to run an independent school—that it occurs to me what it is. In Boston, Betsy and I could walk the streets together, share a hotel room, make love without interruption. Now we are in our familiar roles again, and any interaction we have is predetermined. I cannot just see her. She cannot come to me. We have to pretend to be strangers after we have learned to know each other. I look for her that night at dinner. I am filled with longing. Students at my table talk around me, and Elizabeth listens patiently to them, but I wait with anticipation every time the swinging door from the kitchen opens. I want to see her come out with a tray in her hand, catch her eye as she looks over at me. But she is not in the dining hall. I am certain of it. Just like class, you need an excuse to be absent from dinner. I have half a mind to find one of her dorm parents and see what the story is, though I do not want to call more attention to her than I should. It would be most unusual for the headmaster to inquire about the welfare of a particular student only because she was not at dinner.

As the evening grows later, I find myself in a state of profound agitation. Elizabeth is out somewhere, and I have the house to myself. I nurse a scotch and pace in my office and spend some time peering out the window like a crazy person. Betsy's absence has unnerved me. In my mind I replay all the things she said to me during the magic of the previous night. Was there anything in those words to suggest she might do something rash and let someone know the truth about us?

During the study hall hours, I head out across the soccer fields. The moon is up and hangs low and fat over the river. Between the brick dorms I creep up on her window, but this time I am thwarted. The shade is pulled tightly down, as if she has anticipated my visit and does not want to see me.

I linger outside for a few minutes. I am confused. I try to see in through that tiny margin that exists between shade and glass, but I can make out nothing. I return home defeated.

And in the middle of the night something most curious happens. I am in my bed unable to sleep. The moonlight comes through the window and paints a fat rectangle on the hardwood floor. My thoughts are racing with images of Betsy—her touch, the feel of her beneath my coarse, wrinkled hands. I panic about all I could lose should she choose to reveal what exists between us. And like a school-boy, I also go to thoughts of jealousy. What if I bored her? What if she was disappointed? I think of her saying she wanted to check the box. Perhaps she has expectations, some kind of cliché, of how an older man might perform. An idea born of films or books and one that, I think, is fundamentally unfair. What if she discovered that, when you come right down to it, we are all just boys? Clumsy and stupid underneath a cultured veneer developed over decades of careful living?

I am lying in bed turning all this over in my mind when I hear footfalls in the hallway. Elizabeth. I open the door to my bedroom. The bathroom door is closed, but yellow light streams out from underneath it. I have an urge to confess, to tell Elizabeth everything, though I know this makes no sense. Instead I realize that the urge I have is simply to talk, to hear my own voice in the darkness, and so I go to the door and say, Elizabeth?

Whatever response she has is muffled, and I realize then she is sitting in the tub, as she does sometimes when she cannot sleep. So I begin to talk. And what I say surprises me. You know how the middle of the night can open you up sometimes? How it can make wounds appear seemingly out of nowhere?

And so, before I know it, I have launched into a passionate speech to the door, and to where Elizabeth lies soaking in her bath. I tell her that I am not proud of how I have been, that I know I have been distant, and then I am speaking all kinds of words of love, words I didn't know I still had in me. I tell her I have loved her longer than anything else on this earth. Where did this come from? Welling up inside me, perhaps, from unrequited guilt?

And when I finish I am silent. I wait for her to speak. A moment goes by, and then another. Finally I call out her name, and when she does not respond, I slowly open the door. The bathtub is empty. There is no humidity in the air that you get from a recent bath, no moisture on the windows or the mirror. I have been opening my heart to an empty room.

I do not see Betsy Pappas again until my Russian literature class meets. My heart is practically in my throat
during the walk from my office to the Shephard Hall academic building. As it turns out, she is in front of the building when I approach. It is an unseasonably warm day for
early October, and she wears a skirt that flirts with the
dress code for length. I cannot help but wonder if her
clothing is a response to our dalliance. Does she think she
is now allowed to take liberties?

She is in a pack of students, another girl and two boys,
and one of the boys, Russell Hurley, a postgraduate we
brought in solely for his ability to put a basketball through
a hoop, appears to be holding court. As I walk toward
them, I see the way she looks up at Russell, a tall, good-

looking kid, and how she laughs at whatever it is he has just said. It's a flirty laugh, her head kicking back a little, her fingers once again running those threads of hair behind her ears. She is exhibiting a newfound confidence, and I find this disconcerting.

If my life were a film, this would be happening in slow motion. I walk by them to the entrance of the building, staring over at her. Her head moves slowly up, her eyes stray reluctantly from Russell's chiseled face. Her gaze catches my own, and I smile. She is exactly as I have imagined in these days since I last saw her. I do not notice the other kids around her. She looks quickly away, and my heart sinks a little.

In the classroom she is the last one in. Everyone else is seated when she takes her customary spot in the front. She looks down at her book and not at me when I begin to talk. We are reading Dostoevsky's *The Idiot*, and it is hard to focus. I ask the usual questions—the Christ metaphors and so on—and Betsy seems curiously disengaged. In my mind I keep going back to the feel of her underneath me, my bones on her bones, and then I flash to the moment before we came into this building, her staring up at basketball star Russell, and I suddenly have the urge to punish her.

I can be quite pedantic sometimes. It is a tendency I try to repress in myself. Lancaster students are smart and ambitious, and in the classroom there is seldom a reason to cold-call on any of the students. But today I call on Betsy, posing a withering question, but she fends it off rather nicely, so I come right back at her with a more challenging one. I have a sense of the class moving forward in their chairs. She stumbles a little, and I pounce. It is not a fair fight, and the class seems to sense this. I am overly combative, and at one point, while I am ranting at her, I see a look in her eyes like glowing hate. I back off, and the class settles down. We make it through the remainder of the discussion, and on a whim I assign a paper not on the syllabus. There is an audible groan, and I smile broadly.

"Three to five pages," I say. "Due next Monday."

The students all stand up. "Betsy," I say. "Wait."

She stops and turns to face me. I point at the departing students, and she honors me by waiting until we are alone to say, "What do you want?"

Still, she says it a bit loudly for my taste, and for a moment I do not say anything. "When I can see you?"

"In class three times a week," she says.

I smile. "I am sorry about that," I say, referring to my earlier grilling of her. "Been a long few days."

"Wasn't very nice."

"I know. My apologies. You are absolutely right."

She softens a bit. I can see it in her green eyes, the anger receding. She is a tricky one, this Betsy. Different from any other girl I have known, and yet I feel somehow that I have known her forever.

"This isn't a good idea, you know," she says.

"Oh, it's a perfectly good idea," I say. "We need to be . . . discreet."

"I'm late for history," she says.

"Let me give you my personal e-mail," I tell her. "You can let me know. We'll sneak out or something." It embarrasses me to say this last part, but I am just another schoolboy here, searching for the right language.

"Later, okay?" she says, and just like that she is gone.

That night I drink way too much. Lancaster has always given me the freedom to live my life, you see, but suddenly it feels like a prison. My heart is open to all possibilities, but not all possibilities are available to me. I seal myself from Elizabeth, who now and again I hear in her room readying herself for bed. And Betsy I cannot reach.

That Wednesday is an away day for sports, all the teams at Groton. This is normally a day when I take advantage of a campus largely devoid of students to catch up on development work and many of the other duties that fall on a head of school. But today I decide to make the trip and I drive myself down to Massachusetts. I cut off any surprise Mrs. LaForge may feel about this impulsive decision by explaining that I have just gotten word that a parent I want to meet is planning to attend the boys' soccer game. Old

Boston money, Mrs. LaForge, I say, and there is nothing else I need to tell her. In truth, this is entirely plausible and why I have traveled in the past.

I have no interest in boys' soccer. It is girls' field hockey I come to watch. The game itself is rather silly—girls with sticks trying to give this hard ball some direction but mostly flailing at it, and now and again a semblance of something that looks orchestrated emerges—but on this warm Wednesday in the fall, with the backdrop of the brick buildings and the woods beyond them, it is a pleasure to watch. Girls in their black skirts and high socks and tight white shirts moving effortlessly on a field so richly green it looks painted.

And there, of course, is my girl. She is an okay player, and what she lacks in natural talent or speed she makes up in enthusiasm. She is quick to the ball. She is not afraid of contact. She swings with might and verve.

Mostly, though, it is wonderful to be able to stare at her unfettered. I do not care about the game itself or the other players. They might as well all be props for the one who has my undivided attention. I like the way she runs. You can tell a lot about a girl by how she runs. It is not that she is pure grace in motion, for she is not, but there is something about the flap of her skirt against her strong legs, her ponytailed hair bouncing against her neck, the slight heave of her breasts underneath the cotton of her jersey, the grimace on her face when she is exerting her-self completely, that speaks to me.

She knows I am here. At the half, I catch her in the huddle staring over at where I stand making small talk with some of the Groton parents. Word must have gotten out that I am on campus, for after a time my counterpart shows up, and we trade shop talk and pleasantries. We have known each other for a long time. We are not friends. When he departs with an excuse of boys' soccer calling, I both understand and am grateful, for I can turn my attention back to Betsy.

When the game ends, I pull Betsy from the line of girls shaking hands. She looks annoyed at me, and for a moment we just stand on the green grass, and her teammates look back at me curiously as they begin to walk toward the gymnasium and their showers. Ms. Locke, the field hockey coach, gives me a puzzled if deferential look, and I say to her over Betsy's shoulder, "It'll be just a minute, Ms. Locke."

I am taking risks. The once-crowded field is empty, and it is just the two of us. Some fifty yards away is the stately administrative building, with its brick and broad pillars and the golden dome on top. The windows look like they might have eyes. I take Betsy by the arm, and she says, "They're waiting for me."

We walk briskly toward the woods at the edge of the

field. Betsy wants to bolt. I slide my arm around her as we enter the trees, and it is like trying to hold a wild rabbit to get her to come with me.

Oh, I want you to know that I do not force her to do anything she does not want to do. When it comes right down to it, she is more than willing, and is even enjoying the brazen nature of this adventure. She is not like other students, you see. Her eyes are more open to the world, and perhaps this is why I am so taken with her. She has a sense of who she is that is usually earned over decades and decades of having your heart broken by the ceaseless beat of time.

In the soft piney woods I find a bare spot of forest floor, and on a bed of needles I lay my trench coat down and her on top of it. Her sweat smells sweet, and there is a hint of salt when my lips touch the soft hollow of her throat. We do not undress. We are as furtive as animals. When it is over, I want to hold her, but there is no time. She picks herself up and untangles a twig from her hair.

"I have to go," she says.

I nod. She takes one last look at me where I lie pathetically on the ground, my pants down around my knees. She breaks into a run, and I watch her until she disappears between two large trees.

W hat do you think she saw in you?"

"What do you mean?"

"Just that you are, what, fiftysomething, and she is eighteen?"

"Yes, eighteen."

"Well, that isn't typical, right? Wouldn't she be attracted to someone, I don't know, closer to her in age?"

"You say attraction. What you mean is love."

"She loved you?"

"Of course."

"How do you know?"

He shrugs. It's an inane question. "How do you know your wife loves you? Or your children?"

The man sits back in the chair. He has a pen that he drums lightly on the desk, and he pauses for a moment and looks up at *the caged light that hangs from the ceiling.* "Okay. So she loved you. How do you explain it?"

"I've been trying to figure that out my whole life."

"Wait a minute. I'm confused. Your whole life? This happened just last year, yes?"

"Can I have more coffee?"

"You sure drink a lot of coffee."

"It's warm."

The other man, the one who doesn't talk, stands up and takes the mug off the table and leaves the room.

"But you said your whole life. What did you mean?"

"I don't know. I guess I'm just tired."

"Let's take a break."

"No."

"You want to continue?"

"What choice do I have? I have to tell you eventually."

"That's true."

"We go on, then."

"Please, continue."

The days merge into one, and there is a period of disquieting loneliness after we make love in the woods at the venerable Groton School. I do not see her. She skips my class first once and then twice. She doesn't appear at lunch or dinner. I spend more time than usual walking around campus, but still I do not see her. I am losing my mind, to tell you the truth. I cannot think of anything else. I go through the motions of waking and dressing, sleepwalking through the meetings and phone calls that are supposed to be the substance of a life.

One afternoon I run into her dorm parent and inquire about Betsy, using the fact that she has not been in class to cover the nature of my interest. He tells me she is in the infirmary and may have mono, though he is not sure.

The infirmary is a nondescript one-story building on the edge of campus. The school nurses straighten up when I come in, and I do not blame them, for I cannot remember a time when I have shown up at the infirmary unannounced. I tell them I am there to see Betsy Pappas, and one of the advantages of being head of school is that no one questions you, even if your visiting a sick student is unheard of.

Betsy is in a hospital bed in a small room in the back. The shades are drawn, and though it is a bright, sunny day, it is dark in here. She is asleep when I come in, and I walk quietly to her bedside. She lies on her back, but her head is turned on the pillow, away from me. Her hair is down and messy where it falls against her shoulders. She has on a white hospital gown, and the covers come up and over her breasts. I sit down on the edge of her bed, and my weight shifts the mattress. She turns her head and opens her eyes.

She blinks for a moment as if trying to figure out who I am, and my heart goes out to the poor thing. She clearly is not well. You can see it in her heavy eyes and in the pallor of her skin.

"Hi," I say. "It's okay."

She looks up at me. "Why are you here?" she says.

"That's a silly question," I say. "I am here for you."

"This has to end."

"What does?"

"Us."

I shake my head. Her hand is next to me, limp against her side. I reach out and take it in my own. She squirms it away.

"Listen to me," I say. "You need to get better, okay? First things first. There will be lots of time for us."

"You're fucked," she says rather loudly.

"Betsy, please," I say. "Lower your voice."

"What? You don't want them to hear about us? You don't want all of them to hear about us?"

"Now, now," I say. "I see I have made a mistake. You are not well."

"You remember what you said after you fucked me in the hotel?"

"No reason to talk like that."

"Do you remember what you said? You said, 'You can't fall in love with me.'"

"People say all kinds of things."

"They do, do they? Well, I am not in love with you. It was fun. It was . . . interesting. But that's it. I checked the box, remember? I am done checking it."

"So this is it, then," I say. "This is where it ends."

She looks up at me with those green eyes. She is even lovelier when she is mad, if that is possible. There is iron in those eyes. "Yes," she says.

I search for something to say, something to slow her down. I say, "What are they telling you about your illness?"

She says, "Walking pneumonia probably. Mostly I just wanted to disappear."

"It's a beautiful day. Do you want some light in here?"

"I like it dark."

I am at a loss. "Well," I say after a long pause, "we will speak again."

Betsy rolls her head away from me on the pillow. She stares toward the dark wall and the windows with the shades drawn. I slowly rise and walk out of the room, past the nurses, who say, "Good-bye, Mr. Winthrop," and back out into the bright light of my campus.

W ork is palliative. For a time things are normal. The second weekend of October, our Board of Trustees arrives on campus for two days of meetings. There are thirty-four trustees, and many names you would recognize. The board meets four times a year, and for a head of school these are among the most important of events. Like it or not, the board is your boss. Its first and greatest responsibility is the hiring or firing of the head, and while I am the institution in many ways, I do not take this for granted.

The trustees come in on Saturday, and during the day they partake of sporting events and then they have committee meetings in the afternoon. I generally attend the Finance Committee and the Development Committee, which for mature schools are the most important meetings. Then we have a cocktail party and we dine together off campus. On Sunday we meet most of the day.

This meeting should not have been different from any other, except for the fact that Dick Ives schedules a meeting of the Executive Committee for Saturday afternoon, and this is most unusual indeed. The Executive Committee is made of up of the five most prominent members of the board. It meets by phone in between board meetings and has the authority to act on behalf of the board in unusual circumstances, though, for a school as stable as Lancaster, I cannot remember a time when this has happened. Mostly, it receives advance updates on all the critical things happening at school, and provides me with some general guidance on the broad issues of the day.

The fact that I am not aware of this meeting ahead of time has me nervous and, as it turns out, appropriately so.

We gather in the Oak Room, on the fourth floor of the academic building. It is traditionally the boardroom, with one long table, paneled walls, and portraits of many of the lions of the Lancaster School, including my father and my grandfather. The full board doesn't meet there anymore, and has not in years. It is an austere and quiet room, and on this day, I join Dick Ives, Penny Wilton, Dave Tallmadge, Mark Saltonstall, and Brian Corcoran. These are the school's largest benefactors. The men are all graduates, and from fine old families. The vice chair, Penny Wilton, is a woman with a great sweep of gray hair who vaguely resembles a late-in-life Anne Bancroft. She made her money in investments, some white-shoe Boston firm, and while her connection to the school is local rather than personal—she has a second home nearby—she has become an influential and powerful member of the board in recent years. I should also say she annoys me. I do not like how she constantly swipes that hair out of her face. And she has that particular affect that successful older women seem to develop: her accent cultivated and almost British, her words always far more measured than they need to be.

Dick Ives calls things to order. He was a class below me in school, though he seems older. To look at him, one finds it somewhat remarkable he is still going as strong as he is. He has a handsome, genial face but weighs somewhere north of three hundred pounds. His clothes fit him poorly, and the blue dress shirts he favors stretch around his awesome bulk. He is always eating. Mrs. LaForge has put out pastries and coffee for our meeting, and Dick thoughtfully chews on a Danish as he talks.

"Let me say, Arthur," Dick begins, "That I for one have been very pleased to see you back in the classroom. As we discussed, I think you needed some sense of renewal. And it is good to see the school doing everything it should be. All the metrics are good, better than good, in fact. So I don't think we're talking about performance here per se."

The very existence of this conversation angers me. "Then what are we talking about, Dick?"

"Perhaps I can answer that," Penny Wilton says, and I know then that what I suspected is true. This is her meeting.

I turn my attention to her. She swipes her hair away from her forehead and then folds her hands on the table in front of her where they will stay for only a minute until the hair requires another swipe. "Arthur," she says. "Look, we're all grown-ups here. We know you have been having a difficult time. And none of this is meant to take away from anything you have done for the school, or all the challenges you have had recently. But we thought it was important to sit down and talk. While as board members we are not on campus every day, and therefore not privy to everything, we do hear things. And some of the things being talked about are, frankly, bizarre."

"Well, *bizarre* is a strong word," Dick Ives interjects.

"What word would you use, Dick?" Penny asks.

"I don't know. Look, Arthur, I think you know what we are talking about, don't you? Nothing here is fatal. A lack of focus is all. Completely understandable, right?"

I look around the room. Mark Saltonstall and Brian

Corcoran and Dave Tallmadge haven't said anything, and the three of them look like they would rather be any-where else but in this room having this conversation. Like Dick, we were all at Lancaster around the same time, and they are peers. I consider them friends, though, as in all things like this, I am also aware of the differences be-tween us, that they have the money to live and do what-ever they like, while I have the name and the position, but that when you come right down to it, I serve at their pleasure. And that can be taken away at any time, of course, even though my name and pedigree would suggest that it cannot.

For a moment, you see, I am nervous that they know about Betsy. But if they did, the conversation we would be having would be very different. To the extent there is a third rail in our business, a relationship with a student is it. I am assured that they know nothing about it. Which raises the question, what the hell are they talking about? Who out there is chattering about me? The academic dean who, like all academic deans, secretly covets my position? Some brave member of the faculty? Certainly not Mrs. LaForge, who is far from perfect but who, over the years, has developed the utmost sense of discretion in all mat-ters. It is the most important part of her job, and one that I have never questioned.

Penny Wilton says, "Arthur, let me ask you something

directly. I am sorry if this is uncomfortable, but how much are you drinking?"

I can feel my face growing red. I am indignant. Even my servitude to the board has certain limits. "Friends," I say, my voice rising a little bit. "If there is something concrete related to school you would like to discuss, then I am happy to do it. But a spurious conversation built on innuendo I will not engage in."

"We have an obligation," Penny says, "a fiduciary responsibility to—"

Dick Ives cuts her off. "Okay, everyone. I think Arthur has a point here."

Mark Saltonstall speaks. He leans forward and says, "We all just want to help, Arthur, if we can. You'll let us know what you need, right? What we can do?"

"Naturally, Mark, "I say. "But I am quite fine."

Mark nods and settles back in his seat. He is a handsome man with large features. He is over six foot five. Both our families go back to New England's founding, though I am from a branch that chose to serve, you could say, rather than to lead.

"I think we're done here," Dick Ives says. "We have a busy weekend in front of us. Plus, if we hustle we can make the end of the football game."

Penny Wilton looks positively furious as we file out of the room. Outside on the walk, Brian Corcoran catches up with me. He puts a hand on my shoulder. "Arthur," he says. "I think you're holding up pretty well. Not sure I'd be as strong as you, frankly. And don't worry about Penny. You have a lot of friends on this board."

"Thank you, Brian," I say to him. "I appreciate your support."

We walk together in silence toward the football game. The day is bright, and the foliage in the faraway hills is a stunning mix of reds and yellows. I think about asking Brian what the hell they think is happening here, since all this talk, if they are not aware of Betsy, confuses me. But I know from working with a board for as long as I have that there is always politics. Or, as my father used to say dismissively, the politics at elite secondary schools is so bad because the stakes are so low. Maybe so. I just need to be on my guard.

Elizabeth does not attend any of the board functions with me. She used to be a staple at the Saturday night dinner and cocktail party. She never enjoyed the banal conversation, and in recent years she just stopped coming. I know there is an expectation at some schools that the wife be an extension of the head, always on his arm, perhaps hosting some events in her own right. Some of the other elites have even begun to provide the head's spouse with a salary and a budget for just such work. As if it were the White House.

That is the new model, if you will. Elizabeth and I do things the old-fashioned way. She's always had her own position at school, her own interests. Nowadays they hire heads who do not even come with a history of the school or come out of the faculty. They are mercenaries, you see, who know only how to cut costs and raise money. They will gladly switch ties for the right paycheck. The whole thing sickens me.

Nevertheless, one of the advantages of having Elizabeth at my side is that she is accomplished at moderating my behavior. No more wine, dear, she would say, and like the loyal boy, I would obey. Now, you would think, given the tenor of the conversation earlier this afternoon, that I would be on my best behavior, but the whole thing is nagging at me, and looking across the cocktail party at Penny Wilton whispering in the ear of Dick Ives, I see conspiracy all around me, and in truth, I drink more than I should. The glasses of wine cannot be refilled fast enough, and by the time we sit down for dinner I am pretty much in my cups.

I manage to dump a full glass of red across my table, sending Dick Ives's wife, Rose, scurrying out of her chair for safety. I plead clumsiness, but everything is seen through a different lens now, and I of all people know that, and if I don't, it is clear in the look Dick gives me as I do my best to mop up the spill and then signal the waitress for another glass.

I am out of sorts. That much is certainly true. There is a lot weighing on me right now, and while the conversation flows around me—many of the same old stories we tell every meeting—my mind is across campus. I am thinking of Betsy Pappas, and the more I think of her, her pretty eyes, that angled face out of antiquity, the more I look around this roomful of cultured, wealthy people, middle-aged and older, overweight, the more all of it, all of life, seems so arbitrary to me. Why does any of this matter? This in which I used to put so much import? These men on their fat haunches in their tweeds, and their wives with their plump pearl necklaces? How could any of it even approach what I have come to know in recent weeks? How could any of it hold a candle to the feel of Betsy Pappas asleep in my arms in that hotel room? Studying her body while she slept, seeing where her neck met her shoulder, her shoulder met her arms, her torso curved out to meet the embrace of her hip?

Okay, we have no business loving each other. But love has no master. Love has no head of school. It is as fickle as the wind.

Somehow I make it through dinner without further incident. I even contribute to the conversation in ways that to me feel positive. Afterward, we spill out of the old inn on Main Street and disperse, the trustees to the various hotels and vacation homes near campus and I back to the headmaster's house. Tomorrow is a big day for all of us. The quarterly board meeting.

And while I should go home, say good night to Elizabeth and do something to sober myself for the morning, I do not. On the walk back to campus I hear the bells in the clock tower tolling, signaling that it is ten o'clock and the end of study hall.

The students at Lancaster have a half hour between the end of study hall and check-in with their dorm parent in preparation for lights-out at eleven. Many of them take advantage of this small window of freedom by gathering in the student union, or taking walks with their boyfriend or girlfriend. Coming onto the main walks of campus, I encounter many such students, and they greet me cheerily, with a "Hello, Mr. Winthrop," but I just barrel along, my head full of wine, my feet unsteady as I trudge.

It is a beautiful night. Unseasonably warm, and above the flatlands of the campus that border the river the stars look close enough to touch. At one point I stop just to drink in the sky. I am on the central path that runs from the girls' dorms up to the main campus. I am so fixated on the magnificence of the sky that I do not see the couple moving hurriedly toward me until they are on top of me, and I hear the girl say, "Keep going."

But the boy says, "Good evening, Mr. Winthrop," and as he does I pivot my head toward them and watch as they pass me. To my great horror, the girl is Betsy Pappas, her arm locked in the crooked arm of Russell Hurley, the tall new basketball star. He gives me a great cocky smile, as if he knows all about me and Betsy.

"Hey," I say, somewhat drunkenly, but they are moving swiftly toward the main campus. I say it again, more of a growl than actual words, but their young legs have already taken them out of range. I can no longer see them. Then, for a moment, near the road, the yellow light of a streetlamp picks up their silhouette. I can see his tall figure, and the shorter one next to him. In the black night it is hard to tell where he ends and she begins.

I wake with a huge head. A pounding headache from all the wine. Lying in bed, I recall a shameful memory from the night before. I returned to the house, drunk and full of misplaced aggression from seeing Betsy with Mr. Basketball, to find Elizabeth curled up in the fetal position on her bed, her eyes open and staring blankly at the wall. She did not look up when I came into the room. I stood there, swaying slightly, and still she did not look up at me. It occurred to me that the catatonia she had been flirting with for months had finally taken hold, and rather than speak to her softly, try to bring her out, try to bring my wife back, I instead spoke to her in anger.

"Are you going to spend your life in this bed? Is that what you are now? It's very nineteenth century, Elizabeth.

You know that, don't you? Should I fetch the doctor to look in on your consumption?"

She glanced up at me briefly, then back to the wall.

"You have nothing to say?" I ask.

This finally gets her attention. "No, it's you who has nothing to say," she says.

"Oh, is that right?" I say, eager to engage. "If you haven't noticed, I have a school to run. Not that you would know anything about that. There was a time when that was important to you, though it has been so long I can hardly remember."

"Go to sleep, Arthur."

I stomped my foot. "Do not tell me what to do. I am not a child. Speak to me, Elizabeth."

"Go to sleep," she says again, and perhaps because she refuses to look up at me, or perhaps because even in my drunkenness I see something in the emptiness of her eyes, something that says I will not reach her, not this night, anyway, I give up.

I go to the guest room and pass out with my clothes on. And this is how I wake: starfished in my suit on top of the covers, mouth dry, full of shame.

I muddle through a seven-hour board meeting, and there are times I think I will not make it. I am soupy with hangover, and when I present my report to the board—an hour of straight talking—it is as if someone else were speaking. My words come automatically, and from somewhere else. I hear them linger in the air, and it feels like magic that they keep coming. Someone else is in control of my mind.

I am grateful for the committee reports, which drone on and on, but at least it is the board members talking and not me. Finally, it is over. Back at the house, I collapse on the bed, and the last thing I remember before I fall asleep is seeing Elizabeth getting dressed in the shadows near my closet, putting on her tennis clothes. No doubt heading back to the courts to hit another hundred or so serves. At least she has left the bed, but what is she playing for?

In the week that follows, I suddenly see Betsy everywhere. In class she is sullen and doesn't participate unless called upon, but it seems not to matter where I walk on campus, I see her smiling, knowing face. Standing in a pack of students outside the dining hall, she beams as she looks up at the tall Russell, and when I walk by I see that their hands are clasped.

She is torturing me. It is as if nothing ever happened between us. In fairness to her, she was clear with me about not falling in love with me. Drinking in my study late at night, I find the images coming to me, and I want both to turn them away and to invite them in. I see Betsy and Russell entwined on the wrestling mats in one of those back rooms in the gym, long a chosen place for illicit lovers.

Russell is on top of her. Her hands are up in his hair; her hands are all over his long, sinewy body. Betsy takes him in her mouth. She gives him the gift that is her. She gives it to him over and over and without a care for what it all means. I hate her for it. I hate him for it. I hate both of them.

I am a teenager again. You think this door is closed to you. You think you will never feel the hurt of first love again, and then here it is, a kick to your groin so swift it takes your breath away. Now, I am not a violent man, but I will confess that I have some awful thoughts. I want Russell to disappear. I take that back—I only want Betsy, the promise of what we started that night in the hotel room. I want to make love to her again, to taste her skin on my tongue, to feel the warmth of her breath, her mouth.

So it is not that I want Russell to disappear, though it is hard to see how I can have Betsy while he is around. Late at night, with a head full of scotch, I have this macabre fantasy. There is Russell floating facedown in the river, his body caught in a small eddy, being repeatedly thrashed against a fallen tree on the riverbank. It will be tremendously sad for our community, but when the school grieves, the head of school must lead. There will be services to preside over. Individual students to console. Most of all there will be Betsy. She will need to heal, of course, though healing can require a guide. I could be there for her. I could commiserate, lift her through this tragedy. A shoulder to cry on, a warm embrace to take away the chill of the dark nights.

The macabre fantasies fueled by scotch and the lateness of the hour give way eventually to the reality of the day. One morning I ask Mrs. LaForge to pull Russell's file and, in my office while a cold rain falls outside the window, I open it and dive in.

Russell Hurley is from Great Barrington, Massachusetts, though not from the money that has moved into that Berkshire town in recent decades. His father is a plumber; his mother works as a secretary at the high school where Russell was a relatively average student. Certainly not Lancaster material, except for one thing.

Russell Hurley shattered every scoring record for boys' basketball in the western part of the state. While Western Massachusetts is hardly a basketball mecca, the sheer numbers are impressive even for those who, like me, have a halfhearted understanding of the game. In his file is a DVD. I take it out and put it into the television. It contains the footage of Russell scoring his two thousandth point in his junior year. It shows a packed house of a small basketball court. He dribbles the ball up the court, and the defenders swarm around him, but he dekes one way, and the ball is like a yo-yo on a string off his fingers. He splits two members of the other team with his dribble, and at the top of the key he pulls up and, with one graceful motion, his body springs into the air and the ball leaves his fingers and spirals toward the basket in one great arc. It swishes through the net, and the game is stopped.

What follows is the stuff high school dreams are made of. A banner is brought out by earnest-looking cheerleaders. It has the number 2,000 on it. Russell, with a big grin on his face, jumps through it. The crowd goes bananas. The mayor of the small town comes out with a microphone and addresses the crowd about Russell while Russell stands off to the side, the timeless athlete. When it is his turn, he says all the right things, thanks his teammates, thanks the fans, and sounds like someone who was born to be worshipped, as he clearly has his whole life.

I turn off the television and read his admission essay. It talks about basketball mostly, though he does say that he knows that the NBA is not in his future and that, despite the interest he got as a senior in Great Barrington, his goal is to go to Dartmouth, and to do that, a postgrad year could make the difference for him.

His references all paint the same portrait: a good, humble kid with a preternatural gift. A natural leader. Someone his classmates all look up to. And on and on.

I am no match for Russell Hurley, and not just on the basketball court. I am haunted by the image of him jumping through the banner made to honor him. While I have never been the sports enthusiast that many of my peers are, I do know the grip it has on the high school imagination, even at Lancaster. Russell Hurley is instantly the most popular boy on campus, and not just among the students. Suddenly conversations come back to me: the admissions director and Mr. Peabody, the basketball coach, raving about this new boy, maybe the strongest player we've had in a generation. We're talking New England championship, Arthur, he's that good, they say. Pencil in thirty-five a game, they say. And they couldn't understand my lack of excitement, but then again, that was before Betsy and during the time I found it difficult to get excited about anything.

I return Russell's file to Mrs. LaForge and walk outside into a raw Vermont day. It is late October, and the leaves have mostly fallen off the trees, except for a few that cling to the bare branches like lifeless birds. It is gray and overcast, and as I walk, the first snowflakes start to fall. They won't mean a thing when they hit the ground, but it is always significant, a harbinger, when you first see snow in the sky. Turns a page on a part of the year. The long dark winter lies in front of us now.

I walk to the river. It is not often I come here anymore. Across are the barren fields of New Hampshire. The river runs slow and fat and black on this gray day. I stare at the inky water. A big stick comes down the heart of the river, spinning as it goes, caught in the current. This part of the river never fully freezes, though it can be deceptive when a membrane of gray-white ice forms over it on the coldest of days. I follow the stick with my eyes. It spins one more time, then rolls toward the riverbank. It comes to rest at my feet and stops moving.

"Tell us about the river."

"What about it?"

"You talk about it, but not directly."

"What is there to say?"

"It's important to you."

"Of course."

"Expand on that, then."

"On why it's important?"

"Yes."

"I grew up on that river."

"Did you swim in it? Fish?"

"Swim, yes. All the time. Fish? No. People did fish there. But we didn't."

"Why not?"

He shrugs. *"We weren't the type that fished."*

"Because fishing was . . . ?"

"Something other people did. What are you after?"

"Tell me about your wife. Did she like to swim?"

"Elizabeth? Elizabeth wasn't a swimmer."

"Did you find that odd?"

"What?"

"That she didn't swim?"

"She would dip her toes in the ocean. But she didn't swim in the river, and of course I didn't, either, after college."

"Why not?"

He shrugs. *"Have you ever read* Madame Bovary*?"*

"Madame what*?"*

"Never mind. It's just that her husband doesn't dance. Charles doesn't dance. I don't dance, either. Or swim. It's not—for a man like me—it's not appropriate."

When I need alcohol, I travel for it. There is only one liquor store in the town of Lancaster, and it would be unbecoming for the headmaster to be in there as often as I require. So I get in my car and drive fifteen or twenty miles, where I will not be so easily recognized, and pick up what I need.

It is on one of these sojourns, up to St. Johnsbury, that a lightbulb goes off. At the liquor store, I buy my normal assortment of a case of wine and a case of single malt scotch, but I also buy a smattering of bottles this time that one would not expect me to pick up. Some rotgut vodka, and something called Mad Dog 20/20, and some peppermint schnapps. All products that must appeal to the teenage palate—the times we have found students with alcohol, these are generally what they have.

That afternoon I do something I am not particularly proud of, though, when it comes to Betsy, all things feel like war, and in war, you see, there is what is euphemistically called collateral damage.

During the sports hour, I take the skeleton key afforded to me as head of school and open the front door to Spencer Hall. It is a two-story clapboard building on the main quadrangle, and as a student I once lived here, on the second floor. It houses junior and senior boys and is a desirable place to bunk on campus.

The dorm is empty, as it should be. All the boys are out on the fields. Out of habit, I stop and pick up a wayward flyer that has fallen off the bulletin board. I walk down the long, narrow hallway, and all the flaws of the building catch my eye. It could use a new coat of paint, and the carpet is threadbare down the middle from all those pounding feet, boys wearing cleats inside, which they are not supposed to do but do anyway. Items for next year's capital budget.

I climb the stairs to the second floor, and here everything is the same. In an hour or so these hallways will be full of rambunctious boys readying themselves for the dining hall. But for now I have it to myself.

I find the room I am looking for: 219. I put the paper bag I am carrying down on the floor, just so I can check the number again against the slip of paper in my pocket. I have the right room.

I key the door and open it. The dorm rooms are all the same: high-ceilinged and stately in the manner of the older dormitories, a solitary window that looks out onto the quad. I go to the window and peer out. The quad, too, is devoid of students. One of the things I love about structure: You always know where to find Lancaster students. Their lives are scripted, unlike those at Exeter or Andover, which take a decidedly different approach, though I know they feel equally strong about the preparatory power of their pedagogy.

This room has two beds, one on either side. This is a challenge I hadn't really thought about. Which side of the room belongs to Russell, and which side belongs to his roommate, another postgrad basketball player, though much less heralded? They both have basketball posters above their beds, and this does not provide a clue. Then I remember that Brett, Russell's roommate, is a point guard, and stands only about five foot nine, as compared to the six-foot-five Russell. These rooms have two closets, and the closets are aligned with the beds. It is in here that I discover what I am looking for. In the end, the size of the clothes determines the fate of the man.

Having decided that Russell sleeps on the left side of the room, I unburden my cache of booze and set about placing it under his bed. The area under his bed is already used for storage, so I find a duffel bag he keeps rolled up under here and fill it with the cheap liquor. I tuck it back deep under the bed and exit his room and then the dormitory itself.

That night, at a quarter to eleven, right before lights-out, the dean of students and I, having been notified by an anonymous tip, arrive at Russell and Brett's doorway. The dean of students, a young man named Marx, enjoys the fascist side of his job, and in a loud voice he announces to the boys as they sit on their beds reading, "Room search." They look surprised but unworried as they stand in their boxer shorts and T-shirts and take their place at the front of the room.

Mr. Marx, whom the students loathe, begins his search with zeal, though he is focused initially on Brett's side of the room. It is somewhat unusual, though not unprecedented, for me to accompany a room search. In my youth I did it far more often, though the job of head of school was different then from how it is now. As I have said before, the position has become much more like a conventional CEO than in my father's era, where you were more the head of a vast, sprawling household. A father to all.

While Mr. Marx gleefully attacks the room, emptying clothes out of the bureau and leaving them piled on the floor, I walk around with a general's bearing, lifting books and papers on the desks, turning around and pacing and studying the boys. They are suffering this indignity with measured exasperation and the look of young men with nothing to fear.

This is taking too long. Mr. Marx has his methods, but as any parent will tell you, under the bed is an obvious hiding spot, and I am losing patience. I move toward Russell's bed, and because, I suppose, I want him to know, I look back at him before I go under there. He is unfazed. I reach under and, with my hand stretching, I feel for the fabric of the duffel bag.

I pull it out, and when I do, everyone in the room can hear the unmistakable clink of glass against glass. Mr. Marx stops what he is doing, and I say, "What do we have here?"

Russell Hurley looks positively puzzled. I unzip the bag. I pull out a bottle of flavored vodka.

"These yours, Russell?" Mr. Marx says.

"I've never seen those before," Russell says.

"This your bed?" I say.

"Yes, but—"

"We'll see you in Disciplinary Committee," I say. "I am disappointed in you."

"Sir," he says.

I dismiss him with my hand. "Save it for the committee, Mr. Hurley."

The next day, I receive two visitors in my office. The first is not a surprise. Mr. Peabody, the basketball coach, comes to see me. Tim Peabody was a few years ahead of me at Lancaster and was the Russell Hurley of his day. A middle-class kid with an ace jump shot. Went to college and returned as an assistant coach and a math teacher and never left. He has been our head coach for twentysomething years, and since basketball has never been the priority at Lancaster—trailing both soccer and lacrosse in import—I can honestly say he is someone I do not think of often.

I know why he is here, of course, though I let him say it.

"It's about Russell Hurley," he says.

"Yes?"

"He's a good kid, Arthur. For what it's worth, he swears the alcohol was not his."

"It was under his bed."

"I know. I don't know why he would lie. It's not like him. But either way, there are more important things at stake here."

"Your team's prospects?"

"No. Though we are favorites to win the league for the first time in a long time. A young man's life. That's what matters."

"What about the values of the school? Don't those supersede the needs of any one individual?"

"Oh, come on, Arthur. Respectfully, we know those get bent all the time. If you're a Mellon or an Astor, you can do far worse than a few bottles of vodka and be okay."

"And so you're suggesting we ignore the handbook and our policies because Mr. Hurley is a basketball star?"

"Not because he's a basketball star," says Mr. Peabody. "But because he's a good kid. A solid kid, Arthur. Good head on his shoulders. This is his one chance, and he knows it. He wants Dartmouth, and to come from his family, that's saying something."

I nod. I look away from Mr. Peabody and out the window to the bare trees on the quad. Another gray day in a string of them. Stick season in Vermont.

"Thank you, Tim" is all I am willing to give him at this point.

He stands to go. "Oh, Arthur," he says, "one other thing."

"Yes?"

"Just wanted to say that I admire how you are handling things. A lot of us are."

I stand up and hike my pants a little. I am not sure what to say to this. While I appreciate the generosity of the statement, it always makes me uncomfortable when subordinates attempt to offer some sort of assessment of my performance. It is a breach of sorts, though I know the intention is good. In the end, I just give Tim a firm nod, as if to say I understand.

She is in the outer office when I return from lunch. Sitting in one of those wooden chairs with the Lancaster seal on them that line the wall across from Mrs. LaForge's desk. Blue cardigan sweater buttoned smartly over a white blouse. Modest gray skirt and flats.

Mrs. LaForge looks up at me. "Ms. Pappas was hoping she could see you for a moment."

I am pleased to see her, though I do not show this. I look over and flash her a quick smile, though it is not returned. "Of course," I say. "Ms. Pappas."

She follows me into my stately office, and I turn and close the door behind her. She takes a seat on the couch, and I sit across from her, in my leather wingback chair. It is so good just to have her across from me, so much nicer

than the classroom, where I cannot give her my full attention. She is not happy, and I know why she is here, but
before we get to the matter at hand, I want to drink her
in. The thing that surprises me about this whole Russell
business is that he could have any girl he wants, I suppose.
Tall and handsome and a basketball star. Charming in
an ingratiating way. Yet he has chosen my Betsy, whose
charms always seemed subtler than those of some of the
other girls. I know how lovely she is, having held her in
my arms, having moved with her on beds as varied as
those in a high-end Boston hotel and on the forest floor.
It is one of the things that has given me the most pleasure
in our relationship: the fact that it feels like I can see what
others cannot. I feel that I alone know her true beauty, that
intelligence that flows so easily out of her willing mouth.
How could Russell, simple Russell dribbling a ball end-
lessly, possibly understand her? This is a folly. She and Russell. If I choose to be objective, I see why, why she needs
this. For, despite her confidence, there is a part of her that
still wants to fit in. She is straddling two worlds: the world
of school, where Russell is a prime catch and awards her
status on campus. Then there is the adult world she longs
to be fully a part of, and all I can offer her there. The difference is that the former she can advertise, while the latter
she must hold deep in her pocket like a set of keys.

"It's good to see you," I say.

"You know why I am here?"

I decide to play coy, for this is a game. "You are struggling with your appreciation of all things Chekhov?" I smile slightly.

"Don't be cute," she says.

"I wouldn't dare."

"You know why I am here, then."

I lean back. I am enjoying this. Her needing something from me. I have played this well. "Why don't you tell me?"

"It's about Russell. I know what you did."

"What I did?"

"You put the bottles under his bed, didn't you, Arthur?"

I laugh. "Don't be absurd."

Her eyes flash with anger. "Russell has never so much as tasted alcohol. He has no interest in it. The bottles were not his."

"He will have a chance to make his case in the Disciplinary Committee."

"Oh, you are something," she says. "Look at you. So smug."

"You are lovely when you are angry," I say, and I mean it. There is genuine passion in her voice, in her demeanor, the coiled energy of her young body.

"You think your Disciplinary Committee would like to know about you fucking me?"

She says this rather loudly, probably not loud enough for Mrs. LaForge to have heard in the outer office, but close enough to make me uncomfortable. I have not imagined Betsy going here in this conversation, and it unnerves me a little bit. I suddenly have lost the upper hand.

"Easy now," I say. "Easy."

"Do you actually believe that getting rid of Russell will make me love you? Is that what this is about?"

I sigh deeply. "We are in different places. I know that."

"You don't know anything about me."

"Betsy, please. So much anger."

"Do not take this out on Russell, you hear me?"

Before she can say "or else," I have an idea. "Tell you what," I say. "Come away with me. To New York. One night. I will show you the city. If after that night you no longer want to see me, I will leave you alone. It will hurt me deeply, but I will leave you alone."

I see the air go out of her. She sits back, crosses her arms over her chest. She looks toward the window, the spindly bare branches of the maple. "And if I do this, will you leave Russell alone?"

"I have not done anything to Russell," I say. "Despite what you might think."

"Give me your word," she says.

"Okay," I say. "You have my word."

"When?"

"New York?"

"Yes."

"This weekend," I say.

"Where do I say I am going?"

"Sign out for home," I say. "No one will question that."

You should see us. My Saab parked next to the Dumpster behind her dorm, a Saturday morning. It is a bright, sunny day, and I cannot remember a time when I felt so happy, so full of anticipation. In my rearview mirror I look for her and out the windows I glance around nervously. This first moment will be the delicate one, her getting in the car, our chance to be exposed if someone were to come by. It is oddly thrilling, the daring of this escape in broad daylight.

Here she is now, in the rearview, moving quickly toward the car with an overnight bag. She is aware of the stakes and peers all around her as she walks. She opens the car door quickly and throws her bag in the back, and I say to her, get down, and she closes the door behind her and tucks herself as best she can into the footwell on the passenger side, her head coming over and resting in my lap.

We drive through campus. It fills me with delight to pass students and faculty, staff members and maintenance people. Everyone recognizes the car and they wave to me, and I wave back. Betsy's face is nuzzled to the right of my crotch, and in between waves, I run my fingers through her hair.

It is with a measure of reluctance that I let her know when we have left campus and that she can sit up. She does, letting her hair down when she sits back, and I watch it cascade down and around her shoulders.

There is something cathartic about taking her out of Vermont. About crossing the river and driving downhill to the splendor of New York. She is a small-town girl, and I try to see all of it through her eyes. The speeding down the Merritt Parkway in Connecticut, with its old stone bridges and stately forests hiding mammoth homes. The first glimpse of the wide Hudson, with its steep Palisades, running massively to the sea. And then the turn onto West Seventy-ninth and the immediate hum of the city, the choreography of the cabs, Betsy gazing longingly at the tall buildings rising up all around us.

This is her first time in New York. And whatever misgivings she has about us seem to be disappearing as her awe of the city grows. I have Dick Ives's apartment keys,

He is in Florida now, where he will stay most of the winter. The apartment is spectacular. It takes up the top two floors of Halvorsen Hall, a grand old prewar building on Central Park West. The building itself is more reserved than its more famous neighbors, like the Dakota, and you might not notice it if you were to walk by it on the street.

Dick Ives's pied-à-terre has long been one of the perks of being head of school at Lancaster. He is there only a handful of days a year now, and the doorman Rupert knows me by sight and is too discreet to say anything about Betsy. He arranges for someone to valet my car, and we walk through the cobblestone courtyard to the outdoor elevator that will take us directly to the top floor.

Betsy marvels at the elevator. It is small and old with a wrought-iron cage in front of the door, but its walls are cased in mahogany leather, and gold leaf runs along the outside of a large mirror against the back well. She gasps when the elevator opens into the broad marble foyer, and even more when we open the French doors to the balcony and, in front of us, in the late afternoon sun, is all of Central Park. It does not matter that the leaves are off the trees for the light is tinged with November gold and the buildings on the Upper East Side and in Midtown catch it in their glass sheathing and reflect it back to where we stand together, looking out and across, and down to the small people striding briskly below.

Maybe, I think, this is what love is. Giving someone the gift to see worlds that would otherwise be closed to them. Is there anything more beautiful than a woman surprised?

Betsy runs around that apartment with discovery at every turn. The piano room with its massive Steinway. The gleaming kitchen with the granite countertops and the windows that look west to a wide slice of the Hudson between buildings. The improbable—since we're on the twelfth floor—Scarlett O'Hara staircase that curls and sweeps up to the master suite above.

The grandness of this place, of the city, allows Betsy to forget the nature of our bargain. She is no longer here against her will. Or to win someone else's freedom.

That night we walk those city streets cloaked in the anonymity that only New York can bring. With the sun down, the air grows cold, and I take her arm in mine and she moves into me and no one gives us a second glance.

We eat at some small French bistro near Columbus Circle. I order for us, a whole roast duck for two, which comes out in a great copper pan and is carved at the table. I order a bottle of wine, and the waiter glances at Betsy for a moment, as if wondering if she is of age, but there are still places in the city where there is discretion in such matters. We drink one bottle of wine and open a second, and sometime during dessert, with the crepes flambéing in front of us, I realize that I cannot keep my promise. I realize that I cannot have her just this one night, regardless of how long we manage to make the night last. No, I need her beyond this. I will need her always. It is good to know oneself sometimes, and in this moment I know this with absolute certainty. It both saddens me and thrills me. Though I am smart enough not to say any of this to Betsy. That will have to wait, but I think part of her knows this as well as I do.

We walk back along the park. I take her hand in mine, and she doesn't pull away. There is a chill in the air but it is tolerable. I love the teeming streets. I love the feel of her hand in mine. I love the hazy night above us, the twinkling lights of the buildings.

Rupert the doorman opens the wrought-iron gate for us, and in the courtyard, before we enter the elevator, I am suddenly overcome and take her in my arms. We move together backward until I can feel the cold limestone against my back. I pull her tightly toward me. My kisses rain down roughly on her mouth and on her neck and in the soft hollow of her throat until she says, "Let's go upstairs."

In Dick Ives's stately living room she asks me, "What do you want?"

I say, "I just want to watch you."

I sit on the soft couch and fall back into it. She takes my breath away. She undresses for me in front of the French doors and, when she is completely nude, stands there awkwardly, her arms covering her breasts. "Close your eyes and let them go," I say, and she does. She drops her arms to her sides and I see all of her.

"Move for me," I say.

She begins to move, slowly swaying her arms, and it is slightly self-conscious, but for some reason this arouses me even more, the slight reluctance she has to let go. If it were easy, it would mean less. At one point she releases her hair, and it comes down and falls in front of her face as she dances.

She opens her eyes. "Don't you want to touch me?"

"Not now," I say.

The truth is that I could watch her forever. She is eighteen years old with skin like cream. There is no beating clock. There is no time. She will never be this young again. I want to remember her like this, just like this, forever. She is perfect.

That night we make love in Dick Ives's shower built for two—or, in Dick's case, because of his considerable bulk, for one. I sit on the wide marble bench, and while the water pours over us, Betsy straddles me and when she moves on top of me her breasts are against my chest and her wet hair whips across my face.

Afterward it is like something inside me gives way and I am almost embarrassed to tell you some of the things I whisper to her while we lie entwined in the giant bed in the dark looking to the large windows and listening to the sounds of city below us.

I am a sad, needy puppy; I am the boy clinging to his mother's apron; I am the teenager experiencing the pangs of love for the first time, my young mind unable to wrap itself around the complexity of the feelings my heart slings upward.

I tell her I love her. I tell her she moves me to want to live differently, to do great things in her name. I tell her I cannot live without her. I tell her that I am suddenly aware of my heart. I want to tell her how long it has been since I have felt this way—how sometimes you don't know you have forgotten how to live until you are presented with the roaring matter of life again, until you hold the heart of another in your own. I want to tell her how important it is not to take any of this for granted, for someday you may end up in a cold house where the silence hangs heavier than a curtain of fog over the river. But I do not say any of this.

What I do say is foolish talk, and she knows it and I know it. But it flows like water out of me, and she shushes me, saying, "Arthur, enough," and I love that she calls me Arthur.

"Say my name again," I ask her.

She puts a finger over my lips and says, "Go to sleep, Arthur."

She rolls away from me. I roll into her. I wrap my arms around her and hold her, and soon she is sound asleep.

For a while I just listen to her. Listen to the rise and fall of her breath, and then I slide away from her and stand up.

Outside on the balcony the wind has picked up. I put

my hands on the railing and feel it push my hair back. I look out into the dark, at the park, and the bright lights of residential towers on the East Side.

I am twelve stories up. Below me is the hard concrete of the sidewalk. I think of Betsy inside sleeping. And the fact is, late at night, the only question one should ask oneself when standing on a high balcony is whether to jump. I know that sounds morbid, and perhaps insane, but when you boil it down, is anything else relevant?

I look straight down. A man and a woman—at least that's what they appear to be from this height—walk huddled together in their overcoats. The breeze that blows toward me is thick with winter. I think about going over the balcony. Would I jump and fly for a moment? Or would I just lean over and tumble like a high diver?

I do not want to die. Not because I have tons to live for, other than this girl sleeping upstairs. The philosopher will make an argument that the truly courageous never jump, because the real courage lies in going on living when you know death is an eventuality. That this is the very stuff of being human. I am not sure this is true. I do not jump not because I am brave. Rather, I do not jump because I am a coward.

What do I fear? I fear a tiny moment in time. A tiny moment that will last no longer than two hands clapping. And it is not that (as they say in movies and books) life will flash before your eyes that scares me, but that it will not. Death is so pedestrian, you see, that when it comes it will not be imbued with the ineffable meaning you hope it will. You at least want it to matter; and to be sure, for some it will. For a small few, it will matter a great deal. But the larger truth is that when we die it is no different from a shoe stomping on an ant. The ant stops moving. The world goes on. The world goes on as if the ant never existed.

Y ou don't talk about your son much."

"No."

"Why not?"

Arthur shrugs. "What is there to say?"

"You were angry with him."

"Yes."

"Why?"

"Do you have children?"

"I do."

"How old?"

"Two girls. They are both in junior high."

"You have dreams for them? High hopes?"

"Sure."

"Now imagine if, just to spite you, they do the exact opposite with their lives from what you hope they will."

"Is that what he did to you?"

"In a manner of speaking."

"Because he went in the army? Some people would think that's a great thing. Serving your country."

"He's my only child. My only son."

"I don't get it."

"I need to stand."

Arthur stands up. He looks down and once again is reminded of his ridiculous clothes. He looks around the small room. He is a kept man, and that should be okay, he thinks, because in many ways that is what he has always been.

He stretches and then sits back down. Sips his coffee. "His mother—his mother worries about him. It's different when you have only one. I have nothing against the army. But the army is for . . ."

"For what?"

"I can't win here. I know that. One thing about being head of school? You learn how to count votes. You never fight a battle you can't win, you see. Let me put it this way, and my apologies, for I have no interest in offending anyone. My son, by virtue of his birth mainly, had every opportunity. He did not need to become me, though it is a good life. But it was there for him, and it was not a question he had to answer until he was older. He chose to answer it when he did, and you can argue that it was his choice, that he was a man, but I cannot forgive him for that."

"To play devil's advocate for a moment . . . wasn't it his life?"

"He's eighteen. There is no choice when you are eighteen. What is he trying to do? Be a hero?"

"You're asking me?"

"No. I am not."

"Your wife, Elizabeth, what did she think about his decision?"

"What do you think she thought? She was worried sick."

"That he might die?"

He looks at the man across from him. He suddenly wants to be outside, and thinks about asking for that. He thinks about asking if he can walk on the city streets outside all this cement, if he can take off these clothes that hang on him like blankets and just trudge through the snow in his bare feet, because he could feel that, really feel that. But he doesn't ask because part of him knows this man cannot understand what it means to desire something as visceral as the numbing cold, the crusty snow as sharp as knives against your toes.

He takes a deep breath. Looks the man in the eye. He says, "What is the only thing a parent needs to do?"

"I don't know."

"Think about it."

"I am."

"The answer is an easy one. It's the only answer. Make sure your children live longer than you do. Do that and you've really done something, okay? The rest is filler."

I return from the city to find Elizabeth alone in Ethan's room, sitting in the rocking chair, staring out the window. It is dusk, and there is not much to see. I do not like being in Ethan's room, and frankly I wish we could acknowledge somehow that he is not here, and therefore this room should return to utility as a guest room. But Elizabeth prefers that it appear as it did when he was a student. It is virtually unchanged from then. His navy sport coats and tan chinos, the uniform of the Lancaster boy, still hang pressed in the closet. There is a Michael Jordan poster above the twin bed. I do not like this room and I do not like that this is how Elizabeth chooses to spend her time now, this and the obsessive tennis that makes no sense to me, either. There is no future in it.

But if you learn anything in a marriage it is when to give up. I used to think that all marriages ran the same trajectory. They start with wanting to climb inside the other person and wear her skin as your own. They end with thinking that if the person across from you says another word, you will put a fork in her neck.

That sounds darker than I mean it to, for it is a joke. The truth usually lies in between, and the most one can hope for is accommodation, that you learn to move around each other, and that when the shit hits the fan, there is someone to suffer with. That sounds dark, too, but I am sure you understand. There are few things in this life we are equipped to do alone is all I am trying to say.

This week I learn that Russell Hurley is, despite his youth, both a better man and a more promising human being than yours truly. He is given every chance to confess to a crime he did not commit, in exchange for leniency, for really nothing more than a handful of demerits that may mean washing the floor in the common areas one winter Saturday morning, but he will have none of it.

Discipline Committee is a crucible. For many kids it is the first major test of their young lives. But Russell Hurley is so sincere in his denial, so unyielding in his belief in himself, that I can see the entire committee bending under his indomitable will, though they have no idea what to do with evidence that is more damning than most of what we see. Not a thing circumstantial about bottles under one's bed.

He is also a big, good-looking kid, and this doesn't hurt,
either. Nevertheless, the facts are the facts and promises are
promises. Knowing what I have committed to Betsy, I ask to
see him in my office after the Discipline Committee meets.
There is still time to turn this around, but I need his help.
You would suppose that, as head of school, I could just wave
my wand and it is fixed. Perhaps that is true, and perhaps I
should take this opportunity to right this wrong, but once
we are into the committee it is more complex than that.
Russell has testified in front of his peers and in front of the
faculty members and Dean Marx and, not least of all, me.

Outside it is snowing. One of the first substantial snows
is anticipated, and what falls as we talk are fat, slow flakes
that stick to the bare limbs of the trees. I plead with him.

"Russell," I say, "Think about your future here. We are
not Deerfield. There is no second chance. You can end
this now."

"By admitting I did something I didn't do?"

"If that's how you choose to look at it."

"So you are encouraging me to lie, then?"

"Of course not. I am telling you to be practical."

"Even at the expense of the truth?"

"Life is a series of trade-offs. Surely you have figured
that out by now."

He goes to the window. I watch him take a deep breath. He stares out at the falling snow as if the answer he seeks were somewhere out there. He turns, and I see him in profile, and it is there that, for only a moment, I see the man he will become someday. An attorney perhaps, thicker around the middle, sallow-eyed, tall but slightly stooped. No longer the lean, young athlete.

I think I have him, but he is resolute. "I won't lie," he says.

"So you refuse to admit anything?"

"I won't lie," he says again.

"Just to be clear, you know what this means? That you give me no choice? There is only one way I can vote, you do understand that?"

He sighs. "You do what you need to."

He leaves me alone in my office.

Have you ever wished you could just get out of your own way? That the very moment when things feel inevitable is precisely the moment when you should question their inevitability?

I know this is a trap. This is a mistake, but there are those who live by principles and those who live by nothing at all. And at Lancaster you have no choice—gratefully, despite the hardship that can come with the consistent application of principle—but to be in the former group.

I get Russell's father on the phone. He is a plumber, and I do not expect this to be a difficult conversation, and it is not. There is no nice way to say it, but men like Russell's father are not accustomed to questioning men like me, and when I am done talking he says, "When should I get him?"

"Russell?"

"No, some other kid. Yes, Russell. Is he done now? Or is there something else he's got to do?"

"No," I say. "He's done now. Today would be fine."

"All right, then. Why do things have to be so hard with you people?"

"I don't know," I say, and I mean it. I hang up the phone.

It is done now; Russell is done now, and I am not the one who sees him off. I do get a look at him moving across the quad with Mr. Marx, on his way back to gather his belongings. The two of them walking through the falling snow to the boys' dorm. It is an old ritual, one that has been around as long as there has been a Lancaster, and I do not suppose it gets any easier, especially when the boy in question is not at fault, which is not unprecedented, but is not an everyday thing, either.

The truth is Russell Hurley had a way out, and he could have fulfilled his promise here and averaged his 27.5 points a game and maybe taken us to the New England championships for the first time in a decade, and in the process have carved his own path south to Hanover and to greatness at Dartmouth College.

But he stood on principle, and so did we. And when two parties stand on principle, the weaker of the two, the one without the backing of history and institution, gives. It always does. It is the way of the world, and I do not make the rules, only follow them.

In the middle of this—and perhaps to avoid Betsy Pappas, since I know her wrath is coming, since she will see Russell's expulsion as a violation of our agreement—I go to see my father.

He lives, as he has since his retirement, in an old house just down the street from campus. It is where, you could say, old headmasters go to die. The house is owned by the school, and it is modest, hardly as grand as the house I call my own. Nevertheless, it is a classic New England white clapboard home with green shutters, and around it are the gardens that have become his work since my mother died. It occurs to me that I have been so desperate, and for so long, to be my own man that I have not sought his counsel perhaps as often as I should. He has sat where I sit, and there are not many of us who can say that. One thing that is unassailably true about being head of school is that until you actually occupy the office, you cannot understand its challenges. You think you do, but, trust me, you do not. This is one of the reasons our fraternity, despite our competition, is one of peership and understanding.

My father greets me at the door. He is not expecting me, and it has been awhile since I was over. Too long, in fact, though that is my issue more than his. What can you say about fathers and sons that has not already been said? What can you say that Turgenev, for instance, has not said better?

"Arthur," my father says. "Come in."

He walks with a cane now, and his silver hair is thinner than it used to be, and he is stooped from age. But even not expecting visitors on some random Wednesday night in November, he is put together as if the board itself might show up at the door. His clothes are pressed as always, a crease down the center of each leg of his tan chinos, his gig line perfect, buttons lined with buttons.

He leads me into his study, where he has a fire going. My father insists on fires most of the year. Even in June. The room is overheated, though my father does not notice. He wears a sweater under his blue sport coat.

"Scotch?" he says.

I nod, and he pours us each a couple of fingers from the carafe on the table next to his desk. His hand shakes as he brings me the glass. We sit in wingback chairs in front of the fire, and I do not tell him why I am here, and I do not have to. I do not just visit, and he knows this.

"You been having a bit of a hard time of late," my father says.

"Where'd you hear that?"

"I keep my ear to the ground," he says.

"The board is a little tricky right now."

"Penny Wilton?"

"Yes. Dick is doing good work. But she's a problem."

My father nods. He looks thoughtfully into the fire. I follow his eyes. It can be a beautiful thing to watch a fire. He says, "Arthur, how much of this is about Betsy?"

I turn to look at him. He continues to look straight ahead. Who has he been talking to? Mrs. LaForge? Have some of my conversations been too loud?

I say, "I don't know what you're talking about."

"Don't be daft, Arthur, really."

"Who have you been talking to?"

"Arthur, listen to me, okay? I want you to listen to me. No one expects you to be perfect. You get that? You do not have to be so controlled all the time. You need outlets."

"Outlets?"

"Yes, ways of coping. We all do. You know the old saw: 'Bottle it up and it will explode.'"

I look at my father as if I am seeing a different man. This is an uncomfortable conversation. I find myself wishing I had not come here. He wants to talk more about this, but in truth I am suddenly not feeling particularly well. I stare at the fire, and his words bounce off me and back to him, and now and again I offer him platitudes as if I were listening.

That night I have a very strange dream. I dream that my heart has come outside my body. It is on the outside of my chest, first as a nub and then fully formed. Though it doesn't really look like a heart; it looks more like a jellyfish. It is a clear, oblong thing that hangs like a limp balloon with works inside it, like you see in clocks. Small machinery that moves up and down, up and down. I am very afraid to have my heart outside my chest like this. I feel like I need to talk to someone about it. I try to find Elizabeth but cannot, so instead I go over to my father's house and show this to him. I expect sympathy and remorse and alarm. Clearly, I am dying. This could happen only to a dying person. But my father simply looks at my

hanging heart and says, "That is going to be expensive."
It is the worst thing he could say. It shows he doesn't understand the scope of the problem. Similar to when he
brought up Betsy, as if he could possibly understand what
it means to love her, as if he could possibly understand the
danger I am in. He never did a wrong thing in his life.
When did he become so cavalier? Perhaps age is getting to
him finally. Maybe he is losing his mind.

The following afternoon I have a most curious conversation with Mrs. LaForge. Mrs. LaForge is not someone to offer her opinion, and this has always been a part of her utility: She keeps her head down and does her work. She is most capable, and in all the years she has served a Winthrop in this grand old office, I cannot remember one time when she offered unsolicited advice.

But on this snowy afternoon, she comes into my office and says, "Can I see you for a moment?"

I put the papers I was reading down on my desk. "Of course, Mrs. LaForge. Please come in."

She walks toward the desk and to the leather wing-back chairs in front of it. She says, "Do you mind if I sit down?"

This is most unusual indeed, but I nod. "Of course." I sweep my hand toward a chair. "Sit."

She sits down. She looks weary and old to me, and I realize it has been a long time since I paid her any attention. She removes her glasses. Her eyes are dark and deep set among her wrinkles. "Mr. Winthrop," she begins. "You know I have always been loyal to you. And your father before you."

"Of course, Mrs. LaForge," I say, wondering where this is going.

"And you know I never get involved in matters that are not my concern."

"Yes, yes," I say. "I know this."

"So Mr. Winthrop—Arthur," she says. She has not called me Arthur since I was a student and she was a young woman newly arrived in the office of the headmaster. I cock my head and look at her with puzzlement at her use of my given name.

"Arthur," she says again, "this is hard for me. I do not know how to say this."

"Speak freely, Mrs. LaForge," I say, wanting her to be done with it.

"I hear you in here sometimes," she says.

"What do you mean? You hear me?"

She looks away, toward the window and the snow, then back to me for a moment before resting her eyes on the carpet at her feet. "I hear you talking."

"I do not follow you, Mrs. LaForge. You eavesdrop on my conversations? Is this what you are saying?"

"No, I do not. What I mean to say is that I hear you talking in here sometimes when you are alone. No one is with you."

I shake my head. "Well, surely I am on the phone."

"No," she says, "you are not. I can tell when you are on the phone. My phone lights up red, remember?"

"Perhaps it's broken," I say, and now I am getting annoyed. "What are you implying? That I am talking to myself?"

"No, sir, not that. I mean, not really. You are talking with Betsy."

So this is what this is about. "Mrs. LaForge," I say, "I don't think you know what you are saying. Whatever conversations I have with Betsy Pappas are between me and her, do you understand?"

"I am just trying to help, Arthur," she says. "You know that, right? I mean, your calling her Betsy Pappas alone worries me greatly. Can't you see? It is part of my job. Part of my job is to protect you. I hope you understand that."

"What I understand is that this conversation is over," I say sharply. I do not need to say anything else. I spin in my chair and put my feet up on the desk and face the wall. I stare at a portrait of my grandfather, at his broad forehead, the peak of his hair, his long nose. On the other side of the office, I hear the door open and then close again.

In the open fields of campus the winter wind sweeps across with great fury, and small cyclones of snow get picked up by it and spin in the air for a moment before settling back down. The wind in this part of Vermont starts all the way up on the plains of Quebec and marches south with the river until it reaches the mountains and blows back onto itself. The students pull their coats tight on days like this, and walk from building to building with their heads down. It is a cruel wind, and on this day, the day after Russell Hurley has left school, I brace against it, but not nearly as much as I brace against the coming of Betsy Pappas, which is as inevitable as winter. She will come. I just do not know when.

I am thinking about what I will tell her. I do not have

much to say, other than to plead with her, to give her logic. Russell Hurley determined his own fate, I will say. You have to understand, the powers of head of school are not fully what you imagine. There are things I control and then things I do not. I do not expect you to comprehend all of this, but sometimes events are beyond even my control. They enter the vast stream that is the history of Lancaster, and in those cases, it is precedent that matters.

I consider all these arguments, though, when she finally shows up, outside my house after dinner and before study hall, there is no argument for me to make. Betsy, as is her wont, creates the terms.

I am on the front walk. A yellowish light comes off the porch of the white house and shines on the snow. The night has lifted, and the sky is bright and star-flecked. The air is cold, and I have come outside as if anticipating her arrival, and sure enough, here she is. She marches up my walk with that sense of ownership I have grown to love about her. When she reaches me, she lets me have it, as I knew she would.

If she finds it odd that I am outside wearing only my dress shirt and chinos, she does not comment, and I do not offer anything. The chilly air feels good, to tell you the truth. What she says is that she knows what I have done to Russell Hurley, that I planted the alcohol, which is true, and that she will expose me. That she will shout high into the air that this has nothing to do with good-hearted Russell and everything to do with my venality, that I am evil incarnate and so on. That she will take me down, and the whole world will know that I have been fucking her. She will, in short, ruin me.

When I gather myself from her onslaught, grateful suddenly for the deeply cold night and the stiff wind that has picked up and gathered our voices in its embrace, I summon all the coldness I can and I say to her, "Who will believe you?"

She whirls as if to walk away, and in that moment the long bangs she has, the ones she is always pushing behind her ears, slip out. She kicks her head back, and the hair moves with her in the dark. I repeat myself, "Who will believe you?"

She comes at me then. I am unprepared for this. For her violence. She strikes me in the chest first, and then her fists are in my face. I step back and move away from her.

"Betsy," I say. "Please. Think."

She steps back from me. We stand in the wan porch light looking at each other. Her face breaks my heart, I find it so pretty. I realize one of the things I love about it is its lack of symmetry. Her lidded eyes are different sizes, her nose slightly off-center—her half-moon Slavic features.

Too often symmetry is synonymous with beauty, and it occurs to me that if we are not symmetrical on the inside then why should we be on the outside?

That perhaps we have it wrong, that, in other words,

beauty should be found in things that don't match, not in those that do.

Betsy stands in front of me breathing hard. I cannot help it, I smile at her. I smile at her from looking at her pretty face, and this is the last thing I should do. She is a wild animal in front of me, all heart and bravado and liquid breathing sentience. I know she will come at me again, and when she does I am ready for her. I catch her and wrap her in my arms.

She struggles against me, and her rage is palpable and kinetic. I feel it in her slender arms and I whisper to her, "Quit it, will you? Just quit it."

She thrashes in my arms, but I just hold her tighter. I lift her off the ground like a child, and she squirms, but I have her arms fully pinned and, like this, I back the two of us toward the front door of the house. If anyone were to happen by, we would be quite the odd sight. The headmaster with a student in his arms, clearly holding her against her will, as if she's some spastic child who needs to be restrained.

The door is slightly ajar, and when I push my back against it, it gives way and I fall backward into my front hallway, Betsy landing on top of me.

She scrambles to her feet and is on her way to the door. I do not hesitate, and when I tackle her, it is with no small measure of force. I am on top of her now, and her face is pressed into the Persian carpet. "Let me go," she says, and

I know in this moment that this is the one thing I cannot ever give her. I will not let her go; I cannot let her go; and while you will rightfully imagine it is for the narrow, selfish reason of not having my entire career tossed aside over these indiscretions, that would capture only a portion of what I am feeling.

For the larger truth reveals itself to me while I am lying on top of Betsy Pappas in the foyer of this house in which a Winthrop has resided in for close to eighty years. She stops struggling underneath me, and for a moment there is just my weight on her body, her face turned to the side, the labored sounds of our breathing coming together. And what I realize is that what I want for her is that most unreachable of human desires. I want her to be immortal. Immortal like the great Russian novelists. Immortal like this grand old school built to endure on the flatlands of Vermont alongside the Connecticut River.

And sometimes the only path to immortality, paradoxically, is to die. For to live with nothing in your heart is a greater form of death. To be able to breathe and walk means nothing if you have died inside. It means nothing if you are alone and without love.

It means nothing if all you have built crumbles the moment you cannot have that which you covet the most.

I carry her upstairs. I draw a bath. Back in the bedroom, while the tub fills, I lay her down and undress her. I take my time, for there is no rush. Her skin is still warm to the touch, her face flushed and pink, and it will be awhile before the blood drains and she no longer looks like herself. This is how I want to remember her. Just like this.

When her clothes are off, I stand for a while and admire her. She has never been lovelier. Her eyes are closed and her arms lay slack at her sides, and there is the subtle rise of her full breasts, the brown nipples, the arched cage of her ribs, and the slope of her belly and the dark thatch of her sex.

Lying there on the white quilt, with her pale skin, it is almost as if she were in a state of suspended animation.

Part of me wishes I could keep her like this forever, on this bed, nude, like some magnificent piece of art I come to commune with whenever I desire.

I carry her off the bed and bring her to the bath. I test the water with my elbow as if she were a child, and then I lower her in. She falls back into it and starts to sink, until I pull her up and settle her head against the back. Then I begin to wash her.

I use the large sponge that Elizabeth loves, and I slowly, carefully, move it around her face and eyes, across her nose and down her mouth, along the long trunk of her neck, over her chest and her breasts, down her slender arms, across her belly, through her sex, along her right thigh and then her left, and, slipping down her calves, to her feet. I then start the whole thing over again.

I do this until the water grows cold. I lift her out and return her, draped in towels, to the bedroom.

I lay her on the bed and reluctantly—for I love her nakedness—dress her. Her clothes seem inadequate for the occasion, and I find myself wishing there was something of Elizabeth's that might work, something formal perhaps, but the ravages of age have made Elizabeth a different woman from when she was a girl, of course, and her clothes would not fit Betsy's body.

So I slide her white tights back up over her legs, and then I put on her black pencil skirt. Next I struggle a little with her bra, but once it is on, I put on her white button-down, slowly lifting each button through the hole, finishing by tucking the shirt into the top of her skirt.

Outside, the night has cleared and it is now bitter cold. The wind is not as vicious as it was, but it still runs right through me as I walk. It is late. The campus is silent and asleep. Dwayne, the night security, is the only one I might run into, but I know from experience that he seldom leaves the security shed, and if he does, it is to smoke cigarettes in the dark in front of it. That is on the other side of campus.

Betsy is in my arms, wrapped tightly in a wool blanket. I hold her like a lamb, my arms underneath the mass of her, cradling her. In my arms across the snowy fields, she is suddenly amazingly heavy. It feels like the weight of her will tear my arms off. I look up and measure with my eyes the distance to the girls' dorms, the dorms my father built, the dorms that meant a Betsy Pappas would be at Lancaster at all. It feels impossibly far, but I remember the old rule about long treks and look down at my feet. I take it one step at a time.

The wind is icy on my face, and my fingers are cold. The ache in my arms is almost too much to bear. But at the same time, I can look up and fix my eyes on the horizon, and there are the winter stars in the sky. I can see the great curve of the earth, arcing away from me, and for a second I have that awareness of movement, the ceaseless, endless spinning that keeps us locked on the ground.

I come down the small slope before the girls' dorms, and the dorms themselves are black in the night. In the far corner, where Mr. Linder and his family live, there is the glow of lamplight in the window. Otherwise it is as it should be: sleeping students, silence.

I am going to the only place that makes sense to me right now. When I reach it, when I reach the river, I stop and take a moment before I continue. I lay Betsy down on the snowy bank, and it is good to have my arms back, the numbness receding up my limbs.

It is dark here, since there is no moon. But under the starlight, I can see where the water still flows in places and where it is still, covered with a light tarp of gray ice. I can see across to where the other bank rises sharply, and then, in the distance, the barren fields of New Hampshire, a darker black against the thin light of the sky. I look up and, for a moment, study the infinite stars. The thing about stars is that we cannot tell, with the naked eye, which ones are alive and well and which ones have already died but have not told us yet.

I bend down and, for the final time, gather Betsy in my arms. I step forward and then take a slight step downward on the bank. When my shoes reach the river's edge, I feel the crumble of ice, and then the water is in them, shockingly cold water, around my ankles and soaking my socks, but I do not care. I step forward again, and now the water is up to my calves. I breathe in deep against the cold.

And then I turn sideways. I want to get this right. She is so heavy. Betsy is so heavy. It takes all the strength I have, but I lean back and, transferring the weight from my right arm to my left, I push her out into the air as much as I can. One moment she is there, and the next moment she is not, and when she hits the ice, the sound is strangely beautiful. The ice is thin, and it cracks immediately on impact. It is like glass breaking—no, more subtle than that. It crumples underneath her like the crust on a crème brûlée from a fork's pressure, and then there is the sound of the water spilling up around her, pulling her down to the bottom of the river.

R eturning from the river to my house, I am aware of every sound. The smallest of things seems amplified now, my foot pressing on the loose floorboard of the third step on the stairs sounds like the crack of breaking ice.

I am curiously calm and want nothing more than to sleep. I want to close my eyes and disappear into sleep. But I know sleep will be elusive tonight, and it is, and I am lying in bed haunted by what took place just hours before in this very house when Elizabeth comes to me.

I do not remember the door opening, but suddenly she is there. It has been a long time since she came into my room, into my bed. She stands for a moment at the edge of the bed, and in the half light I see the length of her nightgown and the outline of her. She moves into the bed. We have not made love in years, and yet, without her saying anything, I know this is why she is here.

"Are you awake?" she says.

"Yes."

She comes into the bed and curls herself with her back to me. It is familiar, and we know just what to do. I trace her arms with my fingers, her skin so different from the skin I touched the night before, ashy to my touch. I wrap my arms around her, and when it is time, we move together in silence with the yellow moonlight falling through the window. It is tender and beautiful, and for a moment it makes me sad, and I know, somehow, I know, that this is the last time we will ever make love.

After a while she says, "What happened to us, Arthur?"

"What do you mean?"

"When did we get so old?"

I look toward the window. I don't know whether to laugh. I say, "I don't know."

"Well, it sucks."

This time I do laugh. "It does."

We fall asleep that way, her backed into me, my arms around her, my face pressed into the nape of her neck. When I wake in the morning, there is no sign of her. I roll toward her side of the bed and it is perfectly made, as if she never slept there. She is gone.

For a while there is silence in the room. Then the man says, "So, you killed her."

Arthur sighs. "Yes."

"Are you sure?"

"Have you been listening to me?"

"Yes, of course we have. How did she die?"

"I suffocated her."

"How do you know that?"

He shrugs.

"Is there more to it?"

"There is always more to it. But not now. I am tired."

He puts his head down on the desk then, and it feels good, having his head down. The desk is not wood but some kind of fake wood, and there is something cool about it, like when you put your head against the cool porcelain of a toilet when vomiting.

He thinks, I have nothing more to say. But now that they know the truth they will not let me go. Maybe he has erred, though there is only one story to tell and it needed to be told. He lifts his head as the man who does all the talking says, "There is someone we think you should meet."

"Who?"

"He's an attorney."

"I don't want a lawyer."

"He's not your lawyer. He's . . . he's not going to be your lawyer. He just is a lawyer."

"I don't care to meet him."

"He came down here to see you. We'll just bring him in for a moment, okay?"

He turns then, the man who does all the talking does, and all it takes is for him to turn and a moment later the door opens. A man comes in the room, late middle-aged, tall, a thick head of gray hair brushed back from a full, wide face. He wears a suit, a nice one, Arthur notices, though it doesn't fit him particularly well.

"Hello, Arthur," the new man, the lawyer, says, and he looks up at him, and suddenly there is a flicker of remembrance, and he knows he knows this man but he cannot put a finger on how.

"Hello," he says.

"Do you know who I am?"

"No," he says. "I do not."

"My name is Russell Hurley."

He sits up and looks at him. He peers at his face. He tilts his head to the side, as if this will provide a better look. He remembers being in his office and imagining Russell Hurley as he might become when he grew old. Now he is looking at the man's face, and the effect is at once disconcerting and puzzling. Is this one of their stunts?

"The Russell Hurley I know is nineteen years old," he says.

"Arthur," he says. "We were classmates. At Lancaster. For most of a year, until I was . . . until I was asked to leave. We never talked about it, but I think you know why. But that is a matter for a long time ago, water under the bridge. We lived in the same dorm. We both lived in Spencer."

"Impossible. You were a student last year. You played basketball. You dated Betsy Pappas."

"All true," the man says, bending his tall frame and putting his big hands down on the table in front of him. "Except that I was not a student last year. You and I were students together almost forty years ago."

"I have no idea what you are talking about."

"Arthur, Betsy Pappas was your wife. You married her."

EXPECTATIONS

Army specialist Ethan Winthrop, Lancaster School class of 2002, steps onto a dusty road and sees stars. His only crime is that he doesn't mind being the first one out when the Hummer grinds to a halt, for while, outside, the midday sun is unrelenting, inside the crowded vehicle it is even hotter. Ethan opens the back door and climbs down. His rifle is slung over his right shoulder. Everything is quiet. Everything is still. It is whisper quiet. Ethan looks around. His eyes scan the cluster of small buildings and then beyond them to the open desert. Not a living thing moves, and this pleases him. Movement is what they train for. In truth, he loves this moment, being out front, sensing the men behind him without seeing them. All of it is right here for him, what he has been built for, he thinks.

When he was first in-country, hearing a mortar land, the fear ran through him like water. Some men never get over that, but he has found this place where he can go where it all falls away, where things are simple: his footsteps, the heat, the weight of the rifle where it hangs off his shoulder like another arm.

He loves this realization about himself, that there is something in this world he's good at, and just as he thinks this, he steps forward again, and now he hears something, a sound no more than a dull pop—confusing, really, this sound, the IED going off—and when he turns back to look at the men in his squad, there is that frozen-in-time moment when he sees something in their faces, surprise or horror, he cannot be sure. Everything is suddenly soupy. He wants to say, "Hey, fellas, what's up? What is it?"

But Ethan Winthrop has no way of knowing that what they are looking at is vastly different from anything he can perceive. For the surreal truth is that half of Ethan's face is no longer there, and unbeknownst to him as well, his right arm is skidding brightly across the dirt road like a cigarette butt someone has tossed.

From Basra they take Ethan Winthrop to Baghdad and then fly him to a hospital in Germany, where he lives nine long days made less miserable by pillowy morphine dreams. When the time comes, there isn't a damn thing they can do for him anymore. He goes as quickly as smoke. His flag-draped casket joins others on a cargo plane, where it first goes to Andrews Air Force Base and then to Logan Airport, where it is taken by hearse to Lancaster, Vermont.

The funeral is held in the field house, and the crowd is tremendous. The entire student body is there, as are many alumni; the faculty, of course; the trustees; and then the full congressional delegation from Vermont and the governor, who has asked to say a few words. Chaplain Edwards leads the service and even delivers the eulogy, which surprises many, since when other students have died—a car accident, say—the headmaster became the willing repository for the community's grief. This time is different, naturally, since it is the headmaster's son, but they are so used to hearing from him on all matters great and small, it is a bit of a surprise that he sits with his head down in the front row during the entire service, and even more of a surprise when he is not in the receiving line afterward, but instead is spied walking out near the woods, his hands behind his back, his head hung low, like some country gentleman out for his afternoon constitutional. But since no one will try to measure a father's grief, people keep their thoughts to themselves, and Mr. Winthrop is given a pass.

In the days that follow, the grand headmaster's house fills with visitors. Trays of cold cuts and petit fours make their appearance on the large table in the dining room, get brought to the refrigerator, and then returned the next day as if they never left. Elizabeth is ever gracious with the visitors, and despite her lack of patience with being told to sit down or to relax—as if that were possible—she gives in to it for the most part, though it occurs to her that moments like these, the unfathomable trenches of life, are belittled by becoming excuses for people to indulge themselves. The whiskey and the gin and the vodka carafes are constantly in need of refilling, especially for her husband, who suddenly drinks scotch as if it were water. There is no blueprint for grief, she thinks, and Arthur is acting like a tortoise crossing a road: Sometimes his head is there, and then a moment later it is not. The only constant for him is that he now drinks with impunity, since no one dares give him an ounce of crap about it.

And for a week or so, Ethan Winthrop is the talk of campus. He is regarded, as the dead always are, more fondly than he was when he was alive.

Faculty members describe him as a sweet boy, someone who tried hard to fit in, always a challenge for the son of a headmaster. Some of them have been around long enough to remember his father as a boy, as a student, and against the shadow of a different war. His father, they say, was always quick to remind faculty of his station, of who his own father was. Not Ethan, who kept his head down and was, by all accounts, a pretty good kid.

Students and recent alums, classmates of Ethan's, all seem to know him better than they did when he was alive, stories sprouting up out of nowhere, like the girl whom no one remembered throwing him so much as a bone claiming that he slipped it in her on the wrestling mats after the prom.

Then as a week passes and then two, the finely honed regimentation of the school takes over—the bells tolling, the classes, the athletics, the formal lunches and dinners—and suddenly no one talks about Ethan Winthrop anymore.

He is confined to a distant memory, just someone everyone once knew, except in the great white Colonial on
Main Street, where Elizabeth Winthrop has taken to
spending all her free time in his old bedroom, still full of
his life from just a year before, when he was a senior in
high school. Here are his trophies from basketball and
track, his posters, his prep school clothes still hung neatly
in his closet.

In the afternoons, she sits in a rocking chair and moves
back and forth, like some young girl in a group home
soothed by the motion. She looks out the back to the soccer
fields and the girls' dorms and the woods of spruce and
white pine that line that far side of campus before the river.

On the rare times she ventures out, no one talks directly to her; they only whisper around her about how
tragic it all is. A man cut down in his early prime. Such
promise! His whole life unfolding in front of him like a
gilded path, if only he had chosen to take it.

The one other place Elizabeth finds solace is on the
tennis court. She took up the game recently, and there are
a few other women she plays with regularly, women on
the same level, content to get the ball back across the net—
each good shot a tiny miracle. But now she only wants to
play by herself, and for hours at a time she stands next to a
bucket of balls and strikes serve after serve. It is the met-
ronomic thwack of ball against racket that she likes, the

idea that her ancient, tired arm can still summon the strength to go high above her head and catch that ball in midair, stopping time for just a moment.

But mostly she sits in Ethan's room, and when she does, she thinks of him not as the young man who went to war, but as the baby she carried inside her, the little kicker he was that whole nine months, always against her rib cage, rat-a-tat-tat over and over. "He's got some left foot, Arthur," she told her husband at the time, and that was enough to draw a hearty laugh from the normally taciturn Arthur, and that little boy fought to stay in her like he wanted nothing to do with this world, fourteen hours of relentless labor. And Elizabeth couldn't blame him, coming out into all that noise and light, for who would choose that if they could?

But then, after they cut the cord, the nurse brought him close to her face, and Elizabeth just looked at him—his little features, his tiny nose, and his eyes with the glue all over the lids—and who cared that he was all purply from birth, she knew her own when she held him to her breast. He was a part of her more than anything else had ever been.

And Elizabeth desperately wants to believe that she was better for the time she had with him, watching him take those first tottering steps, and then seeing him rushing through the door as a boy and later as a man when sometimes she caught herself staring at him, surprised that this big, strong person was once a tiny peanut in her arms. But the truth is, she's not sure. If she had never had him she would not hurt like she does, and maybe someday it will become a dull ache, but it will always be an ache, and sometimes, in those moments when the slightest of things reminds her of Ethan—a snowy afternoon on the quadrangle with boys playing touch football, their carefree voices melding into one youthful immortal cry—the ache becomes a deep hole in her chest, and she wants to die.

Sometimes she thinks of her life as a series of halting changes, as if she were a train that was suddenly moved to another set of tracks. She has this idea that other people—Arthur, for instance—live lives that follow more or less a straight narrative, as straight as a walk across a field. Hers, instead, plods along. Then something dramatic happens, a monumental decision, and everything changes until the plates shift underneath her again. It is not until the next rerouting occurs that she realizes she has been bracing for it the whole time.

Craftsbury, Vermont, where her family moved when she was five, is, even now to Elizabeth, a place of both singular beauty and stifling insularity. The decision her parents made—well, her father, to be precise—to leave the security of the family business in New York to make life anew among these highlands of sloping hills and grassy valleys in Northern Vermont is the first of these changes.

Her grandfather had started an air-conditioning company on Long Island that soon grew to the point that he was the go-to guy for air-conditioning systems in the city. The company even installed one for the Empire State Building. Her grandfather became quite wealthy, and it was always assumed that her father would eventually take over the family business. He, however, was as stubborn as her grandfather. He was stubborn and brilliant, and he went to Harvard with the bright-eyed idea that he would come back to Long Island and live the comfortable life of a corporate executive. This was in the placid fifties, but things, at least in the underground of America, were beginning to change. Her parents met in Boston. Her mother was at a small finishing school called Pine Manor, in Chestnut Hill. They fell in love. Her mother got pregnant with her that first year, and they decided to have the child. Her grandfather implored her father to get it taken care of, and to get rid of this girl who clearly had no morals. In the end he threatened to cut him off, and her father said to go ahead.

Her parents got married at City Hall in Cambridge, Massachusetts, and with no means of support, they dropped out of school and her father taught himself to be a carpenter, and five years later, with her younger sister now in tow, they moved on a whim to Northern Vermont, where a thousand dollars got you an old farmhouse and a piece of green earth with views of mountains. They had romantic ideas of growing their own food and living off the land. He would build and repair houses. She might get a pottery wheel and learn how to throw pots.

As with all romantic ideas, theirs was short-lived. That first winter, they ordered five cords of wood for the stove that was the old house's only heat and failed to stack it right away. When the frost came, the wood froze solid in the pile where it sat in the yard. Her father would chip away at it piece by piece, removing the blanket of snow to get at it, but no matter what they did, the wind whistled through the old windows and, on some nights, when the mercury dropped below zero, they huddled in blankets in the main room and were lucky if it got above fifty degrees inside. There was no work for carpenters in Northern Vermont. For a time her proud father, who had spent a year at Harvard, cleaned toilets at a local hotel so they could eat. The cars they owned, an old Saab and a Peugeot that refused to run in the rain, more often than not sat idle in the driveway covered with snow or, in the summer, up on cinderblocks with the hoods propped open.

But the second year, her father got a job teaching woodworking at the small private college in town, and things began to look up. In hindsight, it was a happy country childhood for Elizabeth. There were some neighborhood friends and fields to run and play in, and long, sloping hills to sled down in the winter.

There were also books. Books were her great escape, and Elizabeth had her father's mind. Early on, her father made a house rule that as long as you were reading you could stay up as late as you wanted, provided you were in your own bed. She read everything she could get her hands on. Her parents traveled to used-book stores just to feed her growing appetite. The public school in town, where she and her sister both went, had only forty-six students, from kindergarten through grade twelve. School could not keep up with her. She was bored and got little out of it. Instead, she learned from the books that gradually filled her house, and the math and science her father taught her at the kitchen table on cold winter nights, when outside the wind swept across the highlands and buffeted the windows.

The summer she turned fifteen, she listened late at night in her bed while her parents argued. They did not know their words carried so easily from the kitchen to where she lay with her knees up, her head on the pillow, a novel rested, as always, on her thighs. They fought about her. Her dad said she was dying here, that there was nothing for her, and her mother took the position that anything she needed she could get from him.

"She's already outgrown me," her father said. "She runs fucking circles around me. Do you get what kind of mind she has? It's time for her to move on."

It was an argument her father won, as he won all important arguments in their family, and the following morning, for the first time, the subject of boarding school was presented to her.

She imagined it. She thought about being away from here, this place she both loved and loathed. She thought about her friends—in truth there were not many. A few that mattered to her, but this was a town impervious to change, and they would be here. This much she knew. She had lived long enough to know that some would leave Craftsbury and some would not, and it was pretty much predetermined which camp you were in. She knew she belonged to the former and while she did not think she would leave so soon, she had to admit it held an attraction for her. The new. A chance to begin again. To be something else than what she had always been.

She looked from her father to her mother. "I want to," she said.

"We don't know that we can afford it," her mother said.

"You need to take some tests," her father said.

"Okay," she said.

That fall, her father took her to Andover, to Exeter, to

St. Paul's, to Groton, to Miss Porter's and Choate Rosemary Hall in Connecticut, and, finally, to Lancaster, which was the closest of the bunch. She took the SATs and focused her energy on each question, and when the test scores came back and she was four questions off from being perfect, her father gave her a hug, for it had confirmed what he felt: that her mind was as sharp as any around.

Walking around those old campuses, seeing the students, handsomely dressed and put together, she thought, This is a world I want to belong to. In the end, she favored Exeter and Choate, though her mother insisted she apply to them all, but especially Lancaster, so it would be easy to come home on weekends. Exeter and Lancaster offered full scholarships, and from there the decision was easy. One was an hour away. The other was four. This would be her mother's victory.

In the fall of 1973, she left Craftsbury and enrolled at the Lancaster School. Her life had switched tracks again.

Her mother called her Elizabeth. Her father called her Boo, after the character in *To Kill a Mockingbird,* his favorite novel. Some of her friends called her Lizzy. As a child, she did not like her name. It felt stuffy to her, like an old lady's name. A name for queens, not small-town Vermont girls. Her first act upon going to Lancaster was to change it—well, partially. She chose a new derivative. She had settled on this new name the July before she went away to school and she kept it a secret. She wrote the name over and over in her notebook, practicing how it looked. Sometimes she stood in the mirror and said it out loud, and when she did, she imagined herself at the fancy prep school, moving along the walks, beside the manicured lawns, sitting in classes and arguing with boys who thought they were smarter than she just because they were boys. This was the part of going away she liked the best: She could reinvent herself. She could be whatever she wanted. She no longer had to be this girl who lived in a Podunk Northeast Kingdom town in a drafty house with a drive-way full of cars that worked only on sunny days.

And so on her first day, after a tearful good-bye with her parents during which she both wanted them to stay and could not wait to see her dad's Peugeot leave campus be-fore it sputtered to a halt, she corrected Mr. Crane, her dorm parent, when he called out her name at the first dorm meeting.

"It's Betsy," she said, and from then on it was. It was that easy.

Those first nights, she was homesick. She cried in her bed after lights-out, sobs she hoped the pillow muffled so that her roommate, some rich girl from New Jersey with clothes she could only dream about, would not hear. She felt unmoored suddenly and thought that perhaps she had made a terrible mistake. In Craftsbury she had been the smartest girl in town, and while there were lots of smart kids here, there were also dozens of rich kids, and this she was less prepared for: how much money meant. From the moment she arrived she saw that the culture was different. She didn't have the right stuff. Not only the right clothes, but also the right albums and the right posters. She had nothing she should have had, and for a day or two this was enough to cause her face to break out in a way it never had before, and this only exacerbated her sense of loneliness, and she wanted to go home.

But then classes started, and she liked the small classes, and it was different from Craftsbury—students spoke out, and soon she did, too. Sports were mandatory, and she signed up for field hockey and she was not much for sports, but she liked that the choices were made for her. In other words, it was not a question of whether she would play sports or whether she was good at sports, but instead which one she would choose.

But when the clear structure of the weekdays dissipated in the evenings and on the weekends, she felt exposed, and she was painfully aware of how she stood on the outside of things at Lancaster. She joined the other girls who didn't have boyfriends—or invites to the city or ski houses or wherever the campus emptied to on weekends—in the sad TV room with its tired furniture, where they ate ice cream in their pajamas and watched whatever dreck the television spat out. She saw girls on her hall readying themselves for that half hour of freedom after study hall when some cute boy waited for them outside and the two of them would move out together into the darkness. She longed to be one of them. But instead the TV room became her room outside her room, and she couldn't help but notice that the girls in her position were also the outsiders—the foreign girls; the scholarship girls; the girls who had decided, or had had it decided for them more likely, that their Lancaster would be limited to the classroom and the athletic fields.

But then, after she was there a month, something extraordinary happened. She was invited to an off-campus party. A girl, the daughter of faculty members, hosted it. Her parents were away, and the invitations were exclusive, hers whispered to her by a senior girl in her dorm who had never spoken to her before, with the message that if she were to tell anyone else, her invite would be rescinded.

"Why me?" she asked.

The girl smiled. "Someone wants you there."

It was a Saturday night, and curfew was not until eleven. She kept the secret and did not know who else who would be at the party, beyond the girl who had whispered the invite to her. The house was one of the white Colonials down on the main street, and she arrived at seven, just as the dusk was settling on the early fall night. The girl whose parents owned the house opened the door for her, and she was led into the back living area, where about fifteen students were sitting around on sofas drinking beer and smoking cigarettes. They looked up when she came in, but the conversation continued. She felt awkward and unsure what to do with herself. Then one girl whom she had seen around campus, tall and pretty with long, straight black hair, came over to her and said, "You're Betsy?"

"Yes."

"I'm Kenna. Want a beer?"

It was an act of kindness, reaching out and bringing her across the breach, and she smiled and said, "Sure," and soon she had found a spot on one of the couches. Crosby, Stills, and Nash harmonized on a stereo in the corner, and a joint was being passed around. The conversation was about Nixon, and as she listened to the easy, intelligent banter, it occurred to her how much they were children playing adults, mimicking their parents with their cigarettes and their beer and their talk of politics and war.

The joint made its way to her, and she looked at it as Kenna handed it to her and she shook her head and passed it on.

"Hey," a boy across the way said. "You don't smoke?" He had slightly longish brown hair and wore a tattered corduroy jacket. Suddenly all eyes were on her.

"Leave her alone, Arthur," her new friend, Kenna, said. So this was Arthur Winthrop, she thought, the headmaster's son. She gazed across at him, across the smoke, and said, "No. Is there a problem?"

He shrugged. "Nah," he said, "no problem. What do I care if you partake?"

"Okay, then," Betsy said, and around her everyone laughed, and she felt that she had won something.

A little bit later she found herself in front of a large goldfish tank. The ten or so goldfish all seemed to be standing in place at different depths, as if stuck. Their tails wagged like dogs. She was watching them intently and didn't hear Arthur until he was right next to her.

"Do you think we are like those fish?" he said. "And the earth is a tank?"

She looked at him. "Don't be obvious," she said.

"Excuse me?"

"I said, 'Don't be obvious.'"

He stepped back. "Wow. Are you always this tough?"

"It depends."

"On?"

"Who's bothering me."

"Do you want me to leave you alone?"

"I didn't say that."

"Good, 'cause you're sort of pretty."

"Sort of? That's a hell of a compliment."

"I just meant you have nice green eyes."

"You don't do this much, do you?"

"Do what?"

"Talk to girls."

He laughed. "I can see we didn't start well. I'm Arthur Winthrop."

"I know who you are."

"Oh, good, and you are Betsy?"

"Betsy Pappas."

"Betsy Pappas. Where are you from, Betsy Pappas?"

"Craftsbury."

"Craftsbury what?"

Now it was her turn to laugh. "Craftsbury, Vermont. It's only an hour from here."

"Which way?"

"North."

"I never go north."

"You really are a snot, aren't you?"

"Yes," he said. "I guess I am."

She suppressed a smile and watched a goldfish in front of her, its eyes like tiny marbles. "At least you know yourself. Not many people can say that, you know."

"Self-awareness is one of my strengths," he said, and grinned, and she permitted herself a look at him. He had good teeth, a strong jaw, even if his brown eyes were a little small.

"Well, I feel safe here," she said.

"You do?"

"Yes. The headmaster's son. Who's going to bust this party?"

"You don't know my father."

"Would he kick his son out of school?"

She saw him considering this. "No, probably not. But my life would not be easy."

"You mean like it is now?"

162

"You can presume to say that my life is easy?"

"Isn't it?"

He kicked his head back and laughed heartily. She looked at him and then back to the goldfish.

"Yes," he said. "I suppose it is. But you're tough, you know that?"

"I'm just not good at being a girl," Betsy said.

Later he walked her home, and when he left her at the front door of her dorm, she wanted him to kiss her, but she was not going to let him know that. Before he had an opportunity, she stuck out her hand, and he shook it and then shook his head and laughed. She laughed, too, at the formality of this parting, a shared joke. He walked away into the fall night, and she stood there for a while, watching the breeze swirl leaves in the yellow lamplight, oblivious to the rush of girls who moved past her and into the dorm to check in for the night.

This is what Elizabeth does sitting in Ethan's room on those long winter afternoons staring out at the snow-covered fields sloping toward the woods. She considers the past. She measures it and weighs it and holds it in her hand like a plum. The past is everything now, and she understands that this is what it means to be dying: You stop looking forward, instead living for moments that happened years before. She turns them over and over in her mind, things she has not thought about in years, and she can see now how obvious it all is. Every small event begets another one, each one built off the other until you have a chain of events that all lead to this heartbreaking room with the day slowly fading outside the windows.

It is obvious what she saw in Arthur. She wanted to

belong to Lancaster more than anything, to feel the old school run through her like a river, and who better to give her that than Arthur?

The school was not only in his blood, it was his blood, and he was so comfortable there because he had always been there, and because—though he never said this to her until much later, when she visited him at Yale—he already knew he would return and become his father, as his father had, once, become *his* father.

There is a silly immortality to the boarding school life, and isn't that what she wanted? To know forever the happiness she knew in those two short years when she was a student? Not to have to worry about shopping or meals or where they would live? All that would be taken care of. Teaching—even running a boarding school—is another form of arrested adolescence. Even in their responsibilities, they are all playing Peter Pan, the real world something that happens outside these ivy-covered walls.

They are in Boston. She is sixteen years old, and in the school's eyes this is an illegal trip. Well, the first part of the trip is not, for Arthur is accompanying his father to an alumni event and manages to convince the headmaster that Betsy would be the perfect student to bring. After the event, she signs out to meet her parents, who she says are in the city. Arthur's story is that he will be staying with a friend in Cambridge. The ride down for her is awkward, sitting in the front seat—at his father's insistence—with the headmaster himself. She has seen him only from a distance before, and in her mind he is a great man. He must be a great man, for it is inconceivable to her that anyone less than that would be entrusted with running a school like Lancaster.

Arthur sits in the back, and on the way down Mr. Winthrop grills her about her family, her view of Lancaster, what her dreams and aspirations are. It is an interview of sorts, and she is nervous both to be talking to him—looking straight ahead as she does, at the road disappearing beneath the tires—and to know that Arthur is hearing the version of her story she would tell to his father but not necessarily to him. Not that she would lie per se, but she might color things differently, emphasize parts of her experience more than others, but with his father that is an impossibility. The idea of trying to shape her narrative with him she cannot even fathom. She tells it to him straight.

That night, they attend the alumni gathering. From high up in the Prudential Building the lights of the city and the harbor glimmer far below. She is in love with all this, with her clothes and even with the older male alumni who never knew what it was like to have girls on campus and who have all kinds of questions for her, some of them flirty, a situation she is old enough to recognize and even give in to a little bit.

She is worried Mr. Winthrop will want to see her safely into her parents' hands, but he seems oblivious, and an hour later she is walking in the seasonably warm night down streets lined with lanterns, past brownstones with bright windows that loom over the leaf-swept sidewalks. Arthur has taken her hand, and looking up at him, she knows she will sleep with him tonight if he wants her to, not only because she has grown to find him handsome, but also because she wants this passage in her life, wants to cross this threshold that seems to be the final thing between her and full-fledged, glorious adulthood.

On Newbury Street he finally turns and kisses her, and she responds forcefully to his tongue against her teeth, and she is aware of people moving past them on the sidewalk and she imagines how they must look: the timelessly romantic couple thrust together on this beautiful street, entwined in each other's arms like experienced lovers.

The hotel is his idea—there had been vague talk of staying at Harvard with a friend of his from last year's Lancaster class—and taking his arm as they come into the grand lobby with its marble friezes and its high ceiling painted like a Renaissance sky, she feels her heart quicken and a flush come to her cheeks. You are not in Craftsbury anymore, my dear, she whispers to herself, and Arthur leans down and says, "What?" but she only smiles at him. "Nothing," she says.

Arthur negotiates the reservation desk like he is born to it and upstairs he orders a bottle of wine, and she says, "Won't they card us?"

"Not in the room," he says, and then they are drinking wine and toasting the city outside the window, and when they end up rolling together on the bed, she surprises him by not throwing up any defenses, and even encouraging him, taking him into her warm hand and feeling him leap like a fish against her palm.

She says, "Do you have something?"

He reaches for his wallet, and she is both pleased he is prepared and concerned when he turns it over and she sees the ring pressed into the leather, the presumptuousness of it, but then, as if reading her look when he takes it out, the wrapper crinkled with age, he says, "It's fine. Been there a year, but it's fine, see?"

She turns away toward the window, toward the yellowish light of the pulsing city as he takes it out, and when he climbs on top of her, she is prepared for it to hurt, but miraculously it doesn't, and she wants to enjoy it, but that is not possible, either. Instead, she is rather indifferent to it, this first time, and this bothers her, since she has imagined extremes of either pain or pleasure, and the truth is sadly ambiguous. It shouldn't be so banal, she thinks, becoming a woman. She wonders what the big deal is. She likes his weight on her, that much is true, the smell of him, his earnestness as he moves over her. But when it is done, she is concerned that she might weep or break out in laughter—oddly she could go either way—and she hopes that she won't, but then, just as quickly, the feeling passes. A moment later he is off her, and it is like it never happened.

He rolls onto his back. They are side by side, staring at the ceiling. He is breathing hard, and she thinks about this, that he has just done something, something like work. What has she done?

Outside, the sounds of the city move to the foreground, the scream of cars and the cries of a siren. Voices that drift up into the fallen night.

She likes the new her. She likes having a boyfriend now, the headmaster's son, and she wonders if everyone knows they have done it, and while she does not want to be branded as that kind of girl, she secretly hopes they do. She likes the way her clothes feel against her body, and on the field hockey field she suddenly feels self-assured, even though she knows she is not much of an athlete.

In class she sometimes writes Arthur's name in her notebook. She imagines what it would be like to have a life together, and for the first time it occurs to her that Lancaster just might be a magical place. Weeks ago she was a nobody, one of the TV room girls, and now she is in the middle of all of it, dating the headmaster's son as if she were born to it. Where else can things spin so quickly?

Betsy likes the way others look at her. And she in-
dulges herself in the idea of never leaving here (except, of
course, for college), since, walking across campus holding
her hand in the still fall evening, Arthur says that he will
teach here one day, and he even points out with confidence which one of the faculty houses might be his, and
she loves this vision, a house on faculty row with white
clapboards and leaves in the yard. She tries to see herself as
married to him and she decides that she can. She can see
the two of them in their own house, life just like this but
freer. Drinking wine in front of a fireplace. Summer va-
cations near the beach.

After study hall he meets her at her dorm like all the
boys with girlfriends do, and they walk out into the soccer fields and sometimes they just kiss, and other times
they just sit down and watch the stars. They have not slept
together again since Boston. Though when they are kissing he will touch her breasts through her sweater, and it
feels nice, and once she takes him out and tries to finish
him with her hand, but either she is not good enough at it
or there is not enough time, for they are unable to bring it
to conclusion.

On Wednesdays and Saturdays classes end at noon, and
the afternoon is taken up with sporting events. Arthur
runs cross-country, and sometimes her own game is not
until later, and she cheers him on, standing next to some

wooded path and watching him come flying through in his black-and-orange uniform. She likes to watch him run. He is tall and fast, and his quad muscles clench where they meet his knees, and his long hair flops in front of his face as he goes by.

Once, at Groton for an away meet, he watches her instead, and part of her feels silly on the field hockey field, sprinting up and down with the stick in her hand, knowing she is not that good; but the other part of her enjoys knowing he is watching her, that she is someone who should be watched, and after, when her teammates head inside, he takes her hand and leads her to the woods beyond the field.

The light is golden in the late afternoon. She knows what they are going to do and loves the illicitness of it, moving between silvery birch trees until they find a clearing, and he lays his overcoat down, and she does not bother taking off her skirt when for the second time he moves inside her. This time it doesn't hurt at all, and looking over him to the mottled clouds moving past in the sky, she even feels pleasure, nothing dramatic like she hoped, but rather the subtleness of where they are joined, the sense of him all around her, the quickening pant of his breath against her ear.

One night they walk out into the soccer field and sit down on the cold ground. She pulls her knees up to her chest against the cold. Above the trees there is a harvest moon, the fuzzy gold halo around it that falls apart somewhere over the horizon. Arthur has a little flask of peach schnapps. It tastes sickly sweet, but she drinks it anyway. At first they are silent, just looking up at the sky, feeling the breath of winter in the cool air, but when she looks over at Arthur in the dim light, at his hair falling around his shoulders and his face in profile, she has the sudden urge to say something vulnerable, so she tells him she loves him. It is the first time she has ever said anything like this to a boy, and it feels silly coming out of her mouth, and she immediately regrets it when he says it back to her. She has wanted to hear him say this, such a grown-up thing to say, she thinks, but now that he does, it sounds hollow and rote to her, like another lesson they've learned.

But as a harbinger of things to come, he is unaware of her, unable to read her mood or language, and he leans in to kiss her, and she reflexively kisses him back, tasting again the peach on his tongue.

"I can't wait for you to visit me at Yale," he says, and this further punctures the moment for her, a glimpse of the future that doesn't involve this school, which has become as comfortable to her as an old sweater.

"Definitely going to Yale?"

He shrugs. "Never thought about anywhere else."

"Doesn't that feel weird? I mean, Yale is Yale, but still. Don't you want to see other places, think about it?"

"I just want you to come visit me. So we can fuck in a bed instead of the woods."

This annoys her, too. She looks up at the moon, almost yellow in the light of its halo. She doesn't want to think about fucking right now; she wants not to think of anything, really, least of all Yale, which she knows she will not be attending. She doesn't know where she will go yet, and at the times she thinks of it, it stresses her a little bit, but then she forgets it and thinks that this year and next year are a long time. Time is funny, she thinks, for she has

been at Lancaster only for shy of two months, and Craftsbury, a mere thirty miles to the northwest, already feels a
million miles away.

She says, "Have you told anyone about us?"

"What do you mean?"

"You know, that we had sex."

"It's cool," he says.

"You didn't answer me."

"Not really," he says. "I mean, that's between us,
right?"

"Who did you tell?"

He looks away, and she gets an image of his whole
dorm knowing about them, boys sitting cross-legged in
one of those paneled rooms and Arthur holding court about
her, details about how easily she gave it up in Boston and,
even worse, in the woods on the Groton campus.

"Did you?"

"No," he says. "I swear. No. I wouldn't do that."

And the funny thing is that part of her hopes he did.
No girl wants to be a slut, but part of her wants these boys
to know, wants other girls to know, that she is a girl who
has graduated. That she sleeps with boys. That she will
sleep with boys.

Maybe it is Arthur talking about going to Yale, ignoring the present for the uncertain future—or maybe it is
the sense she has that he has spilled the truth about the

two of them—but walking around that campus as fall drifts toward winter, she is aware of eyes on her, and one set of eyes in particular.

Russell Hurley is a postgrad, and everyone knows who he is. He is hard to miss at almost six foot six, with a thick head of brown hair. In some ways he is an anomaly at this old school, for he is not celebrated for the usual things that one is celebrated for, money and connections or academic accomplishment. Instead, Russell is, like her, a scholarship student, though whereas Elizabeth, Betsy, is here because she is smart, Russell is here for the narrower and yet more elevated ability to throw a basketball through a hoop.

He is charmingly unrefined. He appears to own one tie. His clothes are rumpled but not in that classic, intentionally preppy sense. His pants are never pressed. But he is tall and good-looking, and in her math class she finds herself staring at him, and sometimes he looks back at her, and she knows he is aware of her and hopes it is not just because of whatever Arthur may have told his friends about her.

One afternoon she finds herself in the student union, part of a group of friends, and Russell joins them, and there is something about the way the other girls are drawn to him, the boys, too, and it is not just his status as the rarefied athletic god to grace the Lancaster campus, but instead because he has that nameless magnetism that certain people have, an ease with themselves that draws other people like a moth to a light. Russell is telling a story, and Betsy sees how the other girls laugh, and she finds herself laughing reflexively, and when she does, she sees that he is smiling at her and catching her eye.

Afterward, she is walking up the stairs and toward the outside and the wan November sun when she notices he is coming up behind her, and determined not to turn around, she keeps walking, hoping he will catch up to her, and he does, just in time to open the door for her, and together they move outside, and before they go their different ways to their dorms to get ready for practice, they stop in the quad and talk. She can see in his eyes the same look she saw in Arthur's, a look she is beginning to recognize as desire, and it confirms for her what she suspected downstairs in the student union, when he seemed to catch her eye more than the others.

And she is drawn to this. It pleases her to think that she has become a girl to be desired.

That week, she begins to avoid Arthur. He comes to her dorm window at night, and she opens it and tells him first she is not feeling well and then that she has just too much work to come out. The first time, he is okay if disappointed, but by the end of the week she can see his anxiety and knows she has to do this. She leads him to the river this time, away from the soccer field and other couples. The stars are out and arc away above them and beyond the horizon.

They sit down on the bank of the river. The water in front of them is inky and dark, and beyond it they can see the fallow fields stretching into shadow.

This is the first time she has ever had a boyfriend and the first time she has ever had to break up with a boyfriend, and she has the obvious challenge of trying to make him feel good about himself and at the same time to be clear that it is over.

She tells him all the things she can think of, about how next year he will go to Yale anyway and she will not; how she just needs some space right now; that her studies have to take priority and she does not have the time. In other words, it is has everything to do with her and nothing to do with him, and certainly nothing to do with long-limbed Russell Hurley and his wonderful, open smile.

It goes badly. He cries. She has not anticipated this, his crying, and she hates him for it, since he looks shitty and pathetic sobbing into his scarf amid the burble of the flowing river. For a while she turns away from him and is grateful for the dark so she only has to listen to him snivel and choke on his cries. She looks upriver and imagines the falls she knows are up there but that she cannot hear, and to relieve herself from his crying she thinks about jumping under the falls and letting the torrent of water pick her up and send her tumbling over and over and away.

Looking back through the prism of time, she sees Russell Hurley take on much greater significance in her life than she supposes he should for the short span of time he was part of it. She might even say he was the great love of her life if anyone ever asked her the question, since it is the kind of question she figures someone asks you eventually, though no one ever has.

Leading into the winter of 1973, the only thing that tempers the beauty of the thing she and Russell Hurley have is the specter of Arthur, Arthur who seems to be everywhere all of a sudden. Coming out of class, she finds him there, moving silently by her, determined not to show her he cares, and one night, while she is walking with Russell across the fields she once walked with Arthur, he appears like an apparition out of the dark, and she is startled he is upon them, and Russell, with the ease that certain large men seem to have, gives Arthur a hearty hello, and, when he does not respond, turns to her and says, "Don't worry about him, okay?"

And mostly she does not, for she is too busy falling for Russell Hurley. The relationship, unlike with Arthur, is not immediately sexual. He does not push her, and she likes how slow he is going, like some crazy long-drawnout tease, and at night they sometimes just kiss for twenty minutes or so, and she likes the feel of his strong, long body against hers and the way he sometimes opens his big peacoat and brings her inside it like it's a blanket and just holds her to him.

She likes how small she feels next to his bulk. She's never thought of herself as big, though she considers herself awkward and clumsy, but in his arms it's as if the physical grace that promises to make him the greatest basketball player in the history of Lancaster has somehow rubbed off on her.

What she likes most, though, is that there is no bullshit between them. Russell doesn't try to impress her or embellish his life. He tells her it kind of sucks at home, and it kind of sucks at home for her, too, though she has never heard anyone else at Lancaster admit such a thing.

When she imagines the life of a Lancaster student

when not in Vermont, she pictures summers on islands, holidays in the city, trips to Paris. Russell is not much different from many of the boys she knew back in Craftsbury, and while part of her wants to run from that, there is something entirely disarming about his genuineness. And not only does he speak truthfully about where he came from and why he is here, but he also wants to know everything about her. She finds herself talking much more than she is used to. In fact, she tries to tell herself to shut up but she cannot, for he is so passionate about listening to her.

"I want to know everything about you. I mean everything," he says one time when they are sitting down among the wrestling mats in the gym where they have gone to squirrel away and make out before dinner.

"Everything?" she says.

"I don't want us to have secrets. I want to know all of it. All the embarrassing shit. The things you hate about yourself. The things you love. Your most secret fantasies. The stuff you would never, ever dream of telling anyone else."

"Ha! No way," she says.

"I'm serious. And I'll do the same. Nothing is sacred. Everything out in the open."

"Then tell me something about you that no one knows."

"I'm a virgin," he says.

She smacks him. "Bullshit."

"Really."

"Wow. You're not kidding."

He shakes his head. "Nope, never done it."

"I would have thought, you know, big basketball star and all."

Russell smiles and shrugs. "Not that I couldn't have. I just haven't."

"Wow," she says. "Well, I think it's cool."

"My turn. Tell me something about you that no one knows."

She looks across the darkened room and says the first thing that comes to her mind and does not filter it. "This is the only time I have ever been happy."

"When?"

"Right now."

"You mean this minute?"

"Yes. This very minute. This second. Right now."

"Why?"

"Why am I so happy right now? Or why is this the only time I have ever been happy?"

"Both."

She smiles. "Well, I am happy right now because the only thing I am thinking about is right now. I mean, I'm right here, you know what I mean?"

"You mean sometimes you're not?"

"I mean sometimes, I don't know, I get so caught up it's like I can't catch my breath. And when you do that you're not really living. Everything is so . . . so heavy, I guess. Like where I am going to go college? Even you—I mean, everyone here seems to know what they are doing. I'm just here, you know? It's all future, and if it's not the future, it's the past. My family. My mom and dad and little sister. What are they doing? All of that shit. But being here with you it's like it's just you and me and nothing else. That sounds weird, I know."

"No, no, it doesn't."

"You're sweet."

"So why never happy before?"

"For the same reason."

"What reason?"

"You."

"Me?"

"You and me. Don't make me say it; you know what I mean."

It is his turn to laugh. She looks away, and he laughs that big tall-man laugh, the one that starts low in his belly and moves up through his body. It is a laugh she loves, though now it embarrasses her, and she looks away at the moment he sweeps his arm around her and says, "You want me to say it?"

She turns toward him. "Yes."

"I love you," he says, and she leans into his shoulder, where his skin is warm and clean, and places her face against it and she softly bites his neck. He pulls back and laughs again.

"Hey," he says. "No biting."

"Maybe I want to."

"I love you," he says again, and this time it sinks in, more definite than her teeth on his skin, makes an impression even, one that will last, and she allows herself the tiniest of moments to appreciate that this is the second time a boy has said this to her in the past month, though now it feels different. It is not just words, not just the silly words of teenagers, but it's real somehow, realer and bigger than she can imagine, bigger than their bullshit lives and this small room with its wrestling mats piled high everywhere. And when she goes to reciprocate, it is not the struggle for authenticity she imagines, but rather, it flows off her tongue, and she means it as much as she is capable of meaning anything at this point in her life when she is still learning how to molt into adulthood.

"I love you," she says.

He turns his head toward hers, and for a while they kiss, until they realize they are late for dinner. Ten minutes later, walking into the broad dining hall with its high windows and its chandeliers—to eat, paradoxically, fried chicken sandwiches or whatever is planned for that evening—she likes the fact that they are late, that they make an entrance, that the eyes of the school absorb the two of them as they rush in with the winter behind them and their hair tousled. She likes the clear obviousness of their affection. There is nothing to hide.

That Saturday night, they both sign out for home and separately leave campus, and in the small strip mall parking lot out of town they hop the bus and ride together to Burlington. A light snow falls, and they sit in the back of the bus and look out the windows and she leans into him, and they watch the snowfall stick to the trees on the sides of the highway.

They reach Burlington at dusk, and it is snowing heavily now, and the wind coming off the lake is fierce, but they do not care. He takes her hand as they walk down Church Street, and at a coffee shop they drink milkshakes and eat hamburgers and there is something nice about this, she thinks, for he is so easy for her to be with, different from Arthur, nothing enigmatic about him, just straightforward and as wholesome as the chocolate shakes they slurp with their straws and laugh about, looking across at each other, and then out to the street, where college kids and others move quickly and covered against the snowy cold.

They rent a room at a cheap motel on the waterfront. Russell pays the bill up front and in cash, counting the ones out carefully and without pretension. Upstairs he seems unsure what to do, and thankfully the bed actually has a slot to put quarters in to make it rock, and this is both puzzling and hilarious, and it breaks the ice for both of them when they lie on it and he says, "Does anyone actually like this?" as the whole bed quakes with epileptic fervor.

For a while they just kiss, and outside the snow muffles the sound of the cars moving down Battery Street. He asks if they can turn out the lights. She rises and flicks the switch. Back on the bed, she likes how slow he takes it, finally unbuttoning her shirt and stopping so she can help with the bra, and when later she takes him out, she is stunned at how big he is compared to Arthur, which shouldn't be a surprise, because he is a giant relative to slight, thin Arthur, and when she slowly lowers herself onto him, she looks in the half dark toward his face, and he smiles right at her, and she smiles back, and then she quickens her movements, and a moment later the entire bed breaks.

It crashes to the floor with what sounds like a tremendous crash. They fall apart from each other, letting out peals of laughter that start slowly and build to near hysteria, and then someone is pounding on the door, and Russell stands up and he is still erect, and she laughs and says, "What are you thinking? You can't answer it."

She wraps the sheet around herself and gets the door. It is the hotel manager, summoned by the crash, and she explains that they were not doing anything, it just broke, and in the end, he gets them a different room, but the spell is more than broken.

Later she thinks that if she had known this was the last time he would be inside her, she would have climbed right back on top of him in the new room. She would have ripped him apart limb by limb. She would have chewed on him like a wolf.

But at the time they had no way of knowing this, of course, and on the bed in the new room they lay together in comfortable semi-postcoital silence and watched a Celtics game on television, the men running up and down the court, until she fell asleep in the crook of his arm.

A few days later, back on campus, Russell Hurley had his room searched, and under his bed they found an illegal stash of liquor, all kinds of liquor, and this under the bed of a boy who wasn't going to let anything stand in the way of his dream not to work with his hands and so had never so much as sipped from a can of beer.

He knew someone had planted it, and seeing Arthur's smug smile as the student rep on the discipline committee put it in his head that he might have done it, but Betsy was certain of it, though it was hard for small-town Russell to imagine anyone could be so malignant. The headmaster, Arthur's father, offered him an out if he admitted the booze was his, but he couldn't do it. He had too much integrity.

And so Russell Hurley left Lancaster without ever doing the one thing he was brought there to do, wearing the black and orange and shooting long jump shots in front of a packed gymnasium.

He left Lancaster with a long, slow hug for Betsy Pappas, and when she cried and said they would still see each other, he just held her face in his big hands and looked her in the eye, and he knew as well as she did that it would not work, that there was Lancaster and then there was the rest of the world, and once you were on the outside there was no coming back in again.

She starts playing tennis at first on a lark, an invitation that comes from one of the other librarians, who has put together a foursome to take lessons together from the new tennis coach, who is widely considered to be remarkably handsome, though Elizabeth finds something sad in his good looks, in this man in his mid-fifties trying to cobble together a living by coaching high school kids in Vermont and giving lessons to aging female faculty who look forward to that once a week when someone touches them again, even if it is only a strong hand showing them where their elbow should be for a volley.

She also finds something queasy in his demeanor, his awareness of his square-jawed handsomeness and what it does to these aging, doughy, well-bred women.

But the truth is that behind the veneer of all that macho bravado, and the class-conscious sense he has underneath the surface that he has lived a failed life—he confesses to her once that his dream was to be a writer—lives a really good teacher. He knows tennis. And what starts for her as a lark quickly grows into an obsession. And long after her fellow players give up the lessons, she stays hard at them, and not because she wants to fuck the tennis pro—though sometimes, in the shower afterward, she does think about it—but rather, because for the first time in forever she is getting better at something, there is something new to learn, and her life has not yet collapsed into complete stasis at this old school, with her old husband, and her willful son fighting a war thousands of miles away.

And so once a week turns into three lessons a week. Three lessons a week turn into five days of tennis, one day of just hitting without instruction—still at fifty dollars an hour—and free time spent hitting serve after serve, the satisfying thwack of the ball leaving her strings for that square patch of real estate on the other side of the net.

The pro, Todd, spends a solid month just trying to teach her the elegance of a one-handed slice backhand, and at first it feels as impossible to her as learning to play the violin. She cannot ever imagine mastering it, but he tells her just to be patient, keep pulling the racket back and hit through the ball.

And one day they are on the court and it is like a gift, an astonishing gift, for suddenly she pulls the racket back, and the ball returns over the net with the perfect trajectory, low and spinning, skidding on the court when it hits. Then she does it again, and again, and she is no longer thinking about it, just hitting, and Todd on the other side is saying to her, "Yes, that's it, good hit, just like that, again, oh, good job, Betsy!"

She is so elated by this small victory that she agrees with him that they should definitely celebrate, and so she sends Arthur an e-mail that she will not be at the dining hall and instead finds herself at an out-of-the-way pub with Todd drinking gin and eating burgers and talking tennis.

There is a moment, halfway through her first gin, when she suddenly becomes aware of the oddity of this situation, of Todd, across from her in a T-shirt and jeans, and she realizes it is the first time she has ever seen him in anything outside of the Head tennis sweats he always wears on the court.

She has no business being here, she thinks, for she is fifty-four years old and the wife of the headmaster, and she decides that she will finish this drink and then have Todd take her home. But then the second drink seems like a good idea, and oh, fuck it, let's have a third, and when he takes her home it is not to the headmaster's white Colonial, but instead through the basement of old Spencer dorm (looking both ways, hoping not to be spied by a stray student), where he has a small apartment provided by the school.

He is kind enough to keep the lights off, and when she gets over the awful feeling of being naked for the first time in more than thirty years in front of a man who is not Arthur, he fucks her athletically, as if he wants to show her that his prowess is not limited to hitting powerful forehands. She gives in and lets him flip her this way and that, and later it is this she will remember, how he tosses her around, and not how any of it felt, since she completely blanks when confronted with the awesome spectacle of his near-pornographic and quite improbable ability to work through the first fifty pages of the Kama Sutra in less than twenty minutes.

Worse than the sex itself is the fact that immediately afterward she begins to weep.

Todd at first mistakes her convulsions for laughter but then realizes quickly that she is crying and crying inconsolably. He tells her it will be okay, but it doesn't matter. For the truth is she has no idea why she is crying.

She is not crying because she has betrayed her husband, or even because the sexual act itself has reminded her of all the things she does not like about getting older. She does not cry for her son, who worries the hell out of her with his e-mails from Mosul, saying how scared he is and not to tell anyone that. "Tell everyone I am fine and strong, Mom," he writes, "especially Dad."

She cries for reasons she cannot even understand, and this only makes her cry harder. She cannot stop, and Todd is freaked out and keeps asking what he did. She is sobbing too hard to tell him he has not done a damn thing. That this has nothing to do with him.

Elizabeth does not like when Arthur gets in his cups and seems fit to say to perfect strangers that she was the one who was unsure about having children. He presents this information casually, like a conversation one might have about snow tires, and it pisses her off when he does it, but she feels unable to protest. She was ambivalent about it, that part is undeniably true, and it almost killed her, this ambivalence, but it welled up from deep within her, from a place she didn't fully understand. Of all the things to be ambivalent about! Either you want children or you don't, she figured, and for a time she imagined that something was wrong with her, deeply wrong with her, that she could be so indecisive about something so important. It was easier, frankly, to be cavalier about God.

She had friends who said that women know when they are done having children, as if it were hardwired and beyond their control. The women who have one child and demand a second, and the women who have two children and suddenly want them to flow like rabbits.

And then there are the women, like her, who don't know if they even want a kid at all, and with that feeling comes a weird guilt, because what could be more fucked up than not doing what your very body suggests is the one thing you were born to do? It's like turning your back to the ocean for no other reason than that you dislike beauty.

And so she finds herself, at twenty-five, back at Lancaster, living in a small apartment in the same dorm she lived in as a student, though now with a Wellesley degree, a faculty husband, and a job assisting J.V. field hockey and working the reference desk at Gould Library. She is, in short, what she probably always secretly desired to be: a faculty wife.

And in some ways she has never been happier. It is like reliving the best part of her life, though with money and a car and the freedom to play adults. At night the girls in the dorm check into their apartment—so young, the lot of them; is it possible she was ever that young?—and then she makes martinis for herself and Arthur, and she reads books on the couch while he meticulously grades essays, writing in the margins of the little blue exam books all the students still use.

The campus feels like theirs finally, not like when she was a student and somehow understood she was just a visitor. There is something wonderful, she decides, in the certainty that they will most likely never live anywhere else. Arthur has his sights clearly set on the house where his parents live, and like the scion who goes to work in the mail room, teaching is part of the apprenticeship, though he will not admit this to anyone outside the two of them, not even to his father.

She loves the structure of the school year, how it mirrors the seasons. She loves her job in the library, dressing in pencil skirts and cardigan sweaters and sitting behind the desk, helping the young people carve their way through the voluminous amounts of knowledge in the stacks behind her.

She loves not having to worry about any of the concerns of other newlyweds, cooking and keeping house and paying bills—all of that is taken care of for you at Lancaster. It is as if you had all the trappings of adulthood with none of the responsibility.

And perhaps, deep down, this is why she is resistant to the idea of children. It is a fundamental selfishness, maybe, a realization that a child will change everything, and this state of suspended adolescent animation they are living in will vanish forever.

But around her—all around her, pressing in—one by one the other young faculty wives begin to get pregnant. They are almost biblical in their pregnancies, babies begetting babies, all this fertility like the advent of spring in the verdant hills that rise up and away from the floodplain and the small town with its small school.

At faculty parties on weekends, after the students have gone to bed (or pretend to have gone to bed, more likely), she sits on couches with the women while the men smoke in another room. Other women, she realizes, have this incessant need to put their babies in her arms. And when she looks down at those shriveled little faces, those hooded eyes, she says all the right things, oh, how beautiful and so on, and she coos appropriately and knows her social role, but she can't help but wish that she were a man—not literally, of course, for she cannot imagine that, but conceptually, certainly, the freedom not to have this responsibility, other than in the most general sense; the freedom to stand around with other men and smoke and drink and talk about politics and sports and not hold a baby, whose weight is pleasant enough, she supposes, but whose visage she finds not beautiful but rather odd, old manish and sad.

What could be wrong with her?

Though part of her knows that her reluctance is ultimately futile. On nights when Arthur rolls into her and wraps his arms around her waist, pulling her to him (his signal that he wants to make love), she still has him put on a condom. Though, afterward, when they lie in the dark and look out the window to the stars above the river, he often says, "When are you going to give me a baby?"

And while this provides the opening for her to tell him about her ambivalence, to try to give it words beyond the nagging thoughts in her head, she does not.

"Soon," she whispers back, and then after he falls asleep, she considers all the happenstance that led her to this point, back at school, next to her sleeping husband, already a revered teacher of English and destined one day to fill his father's shoes and become the living embodiment of Lancaster itself.

Maybe, she thinks, it all goes back to 1954, when a boy, a sophomore named Augustus Holt, drowned on a warm spring day when the runoff from the hills swelled the river to twice its normal size.

No one should have been swimming that day, least of all Augustus Holt, who could barely tread water. His father was a wealthy industrialist, the owner of Holt Industries of Pittsburgh, and after Augustus's death his significant gift to the school in the boy's name came with a catch: Every Lancaster student would now have to pass a swimming test to graduate.

Growing up in Craftsbury, Elizabeth never became

much of a swimmer. There were no pools, only the short season at Caspian Lake, ten miles to the south. Saturdays when they had a family picnic, she was not one of those who swam out to the raft and jumped off it.

She was afraid of water. She had always been afraid of water. It was not a rational fear, she knew, and maybe it was no more her dislike of that murky lake with its reeds that slid against her legs like damp noodles. Maybe it was that her hippie parents never pushed her to do anything she did not want to do, some kind of Waldorf nonsense where you figure it out on your own and decide you want to learn something when it is time.

Regardless, she made it all the way to Lancaster managing to hide this fundamental fact about herself, and even though they explain the swimming requirement to her when she is admitted, and later when she first enrolls, she never for a moment considers they are really serious about it. What? She won't graduate because she can't swim the length of a pool? Really? Is this a serious academic position for a serious academic place?

It turns out, of course, that it is.

And so she puts it off. And a week before graduation she gets a note in her mailbox from the registrar that she needs to report to the pool at 4:00 P.M. on Friday and pass the test or not walk in the commencement ceremony.

Coming into the steaming warmth and chlorine-soaked air of the Olympic-size swimming pool, she thinks for a moment she might pass out. This feeling only grows when, approaching the pool, she sees that the only other person in the entire domed space is none other than Arthur, sitting on the lifeguard stand with a clipboard in his hand. He is proctoring this. She considers turning and leaving, as he has not seen her yet, but then he looks up and his eyes pass coldly over her standing there in her black one-piece bathing suit.

It has been more than a year since Russell Hurley was kicked out of Lancaster, and she has not been alone with Arthur since. The times she has been at parties and he walked in, she left. The school is small enough that they cannot avoid each other entirely, though they have not spoken in that amount of time. She has not dated since Russell, and while Arthur has—some bubbly, curly-haired sophomore she has seen him with—she doesn't think it was serious. A few times she found herself confronted with him coming down the stairs in one of the academic buildings, and they did not acknowledge each other. Her heart beat fast as she looked away until he clattered past her.

But now there is nowhere to go. She breathes deep—all that hot chemical air—and walks toward him. He does not climb down off the stand. She speaks first.

She says, "I need to do the swim test."

He looks again at his clipboard. All business. "Yes, I see your name here," he says.

"So what do I do?"

"You need to go from one end of the pool to the other. You cannot stop or hang on to the side until you get to the other end. Then you can take a break. There is no time limit."

At the shallow end, she climbs into the pool. She is almost dizzy from the heat and the silly fear she has of water, and the stress of looking over at Arthur, smug on the lifeguard stand, looking down at her, at the water rising up around her and soaking her bathing suit.

She stands for a moment and looks down the length of the pool. It feels like a great distance, a near-impossible task. It is also humiliating, the fact that she isn't a good swimmer, can't swim, and that Arthur is here to witness it. She takes one last look up at him. One last glance to the other side. Then she takes a deep breath and goes for it.

She does a modified doggie paddle, her arms and legs flailing under the water, propelling her forward, her head barely above the water, like a retriever cutting through a pond.

It is beyond humiliating, and she tells herself just to keep moving, push and kick, push and kick, over and over, and finally she looks up, thinking she must be nearing the end, only to realize she has not traveled more than a third of the way. She puts her head down and presses on, and a moment later, she is in trouble.

Her legs, which had been behind her, are now surprisingly below her, as if she has lost her natural buoyancy. The water is in her nose, and she tries to compensate by whirling her arms faster, but this seems to make it worse, and now she is under, closing her eyes and trying to push toward the top.

She doesn't so much hear Arthur, other than as some distant swoosh, as feel him, his arm around her waist, his hands up over her breasts, her neck, pulling her up and sputtering out of the water.

"Easy now," he says in her ear. "Easy now."

At the pool's wall she hangs on to the edge, and he is behind her, saying, "You okay, Betsy? You okay?"

She pulls herself up and out of the water. On her knees, she completes the humiliation by throwing up.

And Arthur is there, whispering to her kindly, sliding her hair away from her face. She turns toward him, and the nausea has passed, and now she starts to laugh, uncontrollably, some great release of tension, and Arthur laughs, too, and when she says, "Oh, fuck, now I'm not going to graduate," he says, "Not to worry. I mean, you went back and forth the whole length from what I could see," and they laugh even harder now, and she is grateful to him.

Time is stripped away. They are back where they were more than a year ago, sitting on the dewy fall grass and watching the stars together. For a moment it as if nothing happened. Time is malleable. Memory fails. Memory changes.

Graduation day comes, and the day, as it should be, is bright and beautiful, and one by one the newly minted Lancaster graduates fulfill the tradition by ringing the bell that sits on top of the small hill behind the main quad. The girls wear all-white knee-length dresses, while the boys wear navy blazers, tan khakis, and Lancaster ties. They are a sea of sameness, and when Arthur rings the bell, Betsy watches as he steps through this window in time like Winthrops have always done and she thinks that the uniform and the moment seem to suit him better than most, and then she washes it out of her head, since she figures she will never see him again. Over the past couple of days since her swim test they have talked a few times, but nothing significant. She has forgiven him for what she believes he did to Russell, and part of her feels tremendously guilty about this, as if she is giving in to the larger forces that are this old school, but she also knows that Lancaster moves forward with the force of a river and that once someone is gone it's as if he were never there. Lancaster has a way of dealing only with the living.

In the fall Arthur goes to Yale, and she goes to Wellesley. That first year, there are a few boys, one-night stands, really, but nothing that ever evolves into a relationship. Boys who tell her all kinds of things to get her into bed—like the long-haired Harvard student who tells her after eating hallucinogenic mushrooms that he wants to fuck her through rainbows.

She doesn't know if he means it literally, and he cannot explain it when she presses him, but it turns out that, naturally, he is so high that the point is moot.

One January night Betsy rides a chartered bus from Wellesley to New Haven with a group of other girls. They are expected at a mixer at Scroll and Key, a prominent secret society, and when they arrive a soft snow is falling on the trees in front of a magnificent granite building that looks more like a monument or a tomb than a place you would actually enter. Betsy files off the bus with all the other Wellesley girls. It is her first time at Yale, and she wonders if she will see Arthur, but she assumes she will not, since after all it is a big school. There are some other

Lancaster boys at Yale but none that she was close to, and that is not why she is here, anyway. Coming off the bus, she thinks maybe she has made a mistake. She has been to only one of these before, at Harvard, when she first got to college, and that feeling she had then comes back now, the feeling of being on parade for privileged boys, their eyes on her, sizing her up in the narrowest of ways, as if they, these Wellesley women, are little more than what they suggest in their blouses and skirts, when around them they face a rapidly changing world where every facet of their education speaks to another truth.

Inside they are led into a great room, and there is punch and Yale boys, and she is not one who draws them but she is also not threatening, either, pretty enough for them to want to talk to her but not one of those girls who gets noticed right away, which she has decided is okay by her. The ceiling is vaulted, held up by great pillars, and there are staircases that lead up from either side to a balcony, and it is on this balcony, an hour into the awkward soiree, that suddenly they hear the sound of singing, high-voiced and pretty, and quickly all other sound falls away, and Betsy cannot at first help but smile at the sight of them, fifteen or so Yale men, dressed identically in a uniform not so different from those she remembers from Lancaster: navy jackets and ties and pressed khakis. The song is funny and ribald, and contains a line about how punch delivers certain properties to extract the chaste from the women of Wellesley.

She is smiling at this display, along with the others, when she notices Arthur. He is in the second row of the singing men. She does not know why it has taken her so long to see him, since he is unchanged, that tall, narrow countenance and the flop of brown hair falling over his forehead. He is staring right at her, and she knows then that he has seen her all along, and even though she is far below him, she can also see that he knows now that she has recognized him, and he allows himself the thinnest of smiles during the song's last stanza.

When they finish, her heart is in her throat, as she knows he will come to her, and she is determined to act surprised, her back to the staircases as if she is scanning the rest of the room, and it is his hand on her shoulder she feels first, and when she turns, he is in front of her.

"Betsy," he says.

"Hello, Arthur."

"You look well," he says.

She smiles. "You, too."

And maybe it is the pull of Lancaster itself, the realization that even after eighteenth months at Wellesley she misses the old Vermont school. Things were simpler then, weren't they? Or at least less formed. And seeing Arthur again, she feels somehow as if she knows him better than anyone else, better than the friends she rode the bus with, better than the boys from Harvard she opened herself up to on fall nights, doing the walk of shame out of brick dorms and into the gray, liquid air of dawn. Is there a way, she wonders, sitting on the granite steps with him, their backs against the cool stone wall, watching people mingle below them, to square what he did to Russell with this boy graciously making her laugh now? Could his actions be seen somehow as an act of chivalry? That, of course, she decides, is a stretch, but at a minimum she can put it away, store it like a yellowed letter in a small box deep in the closet of her mind.

When the bus leaves at 11:15 for the ride back up to Massachusetts, she is not on it. Instead, she is in a nearby dorm, fully clothed, on her back on a bed next to Arthur Winthrop, talking in the half dark, staring at the ceiling, whispering stories with him as if the past were a long time ago.

On weekends they burn up the highways from suburban Boston to New Haven, more she than he, since she can stay in his dorm. At Wellesley things change more slowly, and she has to sneak him in. The young Arthur is an ardent lover, and they fuck with abandon. His roommate—a nice, tall, skinny, long-haired kid from Exeter, of all places—is kind enough to find another place to stay on the nights she comes down.

In that dorm room, with its fireplace and high ceilings and its view of the broad expanse of the quad, they try their hardest never to leave this space. They bring in pizza. They drink wine straight from the bottle. They smoke cigarettes. She studies, and he does not. This mystifies her about Arthur, how he never seems to study. She feels perpetually behind, like she will never catch up, but he doesn't seem to give a shit, or at least that's what he wants to show her. In the end, she decides it's genuine: that he is just one of those people who can absorb books, never take notes, and show up and ace his tests. Plus, he has the advantage of knowing what graduation brings. Graduation brings a return to Lancaster. The point is to get the degree. No more, no less.

College, as it turns out, is Lancaster unbridled, Lancaster without rules.

They can sleep as late as they want. They can be in each other's rooms. They can smoke and drink, and if they want to skip class—something he does but she cannot imagine, aware, as she is, of the dollars and cents of it all—they can do that, too. Most of all they can make love, and in those first months, those precious weekends when she arrives late and they fall into each other, they are as much scientists as they are artists.

She is on the Pill now. It is a revelation, this thing she takes every day that says she can have as much sex as she wants and not worry about getting pregnant. Arthur loves it, too, for it is as if the last impediment to relentless fucking has been removed. Plus, she is all hormones. "Look at me," she says to Arthur once, "my tits are bigger, aren't they? I mean, I'm not imagining that, right?"

"No," he says, "you're not."

And so she climbs on top of him; he climbs on top of her; they climb on top of each other and curl together like vines.

All walls between them fall away, and they are willing to be naked with each other, not just in the narrow biblical sense, but in the larger sense of the word, opening their insides as well as their outsides without shame or remorse or fear. She lets Arthur see her with all her flaws and she sees all of his, and sometimes, when she is leaving him, a wave of inexplicable sadness comes over her. It is nothing specific that she can point to—not the leaving, for she likes her freedom, too—but come over her it does, and soon she is weeping.

Arthur always mistakes this for her having to get back on Interstate 95 and leave him behind, and he invariably commits the one mistake he will compound throughout their lives: a failure to leave her alone. If he just let her be sad, just let her dwell in it for a moment, she would come out the other side and be fine.

But he is a man and he wants to fix her. She tells him not to, she tells him he cannot, but he doesn't stop. He tries humor at first, as if he can jolly her out of this mood, and when that doesn't work he tries anger.

"For Christ's sake, Betsy, knock it off, will you?"

On her birthday he takes her to New York City and surprises her by securing Dick Ives's apartment. Dick is a friend of theirs from Lancaster, and the apartment has been in his family. She has heard of it before, this grand place that Dick sometimes lets his friends use, but she has never seen it.

As a consequence, Betsy finds herself in the most remarkable apartment she has ever seen, the penthouse of Halvorsen Hall on West Sixty-fourth and Central Park West. The place is huge by New York standards, two floors with a swooping staircase that leads up to the bedrooms and, most magnificently, a balcony—can you call it balcony if it fits fifty people?—with marble railings that looks out over Central Park to the towers of the Upper East Side.

This is in the fall. The city is gorgeous in autumn color, and they catch a Broadway show, eat dinner at a French restaurant, where a duck is carved at the table for them and a sauce is ladled out of a copper pan and onto their plates.

They drink bottles of wine and afterward they walk down the busy city streets with their arms locked, strolling while the bustle flows over and around them. Everyone, it seems, is in a hurry except for the two of them.

That night, when they are both high from the wine, she dances for Arthur. It begins as a lark, something funny to do, though she admits she likes his gaze on her as she takes off her clothes in front of the window, not giving a shit who might be looking in from the big city. She likes his gaze as she begins to move for him, closing her eyes and letting her body go, truly go, for the first time in her life.

They make love in the huge shower with water spilling over them, and afterward, now on their third bottle of wine, she breaks down again, this time even more unexpectedly—it comes over her faster than a cold—and maybe it is because it happens after a magical night in the city, the gift of it that he has given her on her birthday, and while Arthur wants to deliver her from this moment, she knows that he cannot and that, like a cold, it will have to run its course.

He goes silent, and she rolls away from him on the bed, toward the wall, toward the window that looks west between the buildings to the Hudson. A few minutes later, she hears him leave the room.

At one point she falls asleep, and when she wakes he is nowhere to be found. She moves through the apartment until she finds him on the balcony. He is naked with his hands on the top of the ornate balustrade. She comes up behind him, and now he is the one who is weeping. The air is cool this high up, and the breeze stiffens her nipples and blows her hair off her shoulders. She does not say anything, but follows his eyes to the ground far below. It is late at night, but the street is full of people. Cars stream down Central Park West toward Columbus Circle.

He turns and looks at her, his eyes fat with tears.

"What are you thinking about?" she says.

"Honestly?"

"Yes."

"I am thinking I would like to walk in the park naked. Disappear into its trees and not come back."

And then she realizes that they are more alike than she has imagined. Like her, he is broken. And she thinks perhaps this is what love is: letting someone else see that part of you that shatters like glass. All of us are broken in our own way. And in that moment, on her birthday, looking over the black trees to the bright lights of the other side, she knows she will marry Arthur. They will grow old together, broken together, and as long as they both don't completely shatter at the same time, they might find a way to pick each other off the ground.

One night they are at a faculty dinner at one of the houses on the row. It is early September but might as well be midsummer for there is a heat wave, and while the wife offers gin and tonics, the husband lights the grill for steaks. They could be anywhere, Betsy thinks, at any old cookout, except that the white clapboard is so classically New England and in the walled-in garden the faculty chatting in small groups are mostly in their late twenties and thirties, a particularly handsome group of people, she thinks, especially in the bright sunlight and against the pale blue sky.

She is standing with Arthur and with James Booth, the new art teacher, and his wife, Ella, who has been hired into music. They are a little different, more bohemian, she supposes, and this is partly on her mind, but mostly she is not listening, for behind them she sees the host's daughter, a girl of about thirteen, sitting cross-legged near the rosebushes in the far corner of the garden. The girl is beautiful, with long, straight flaxen hair, and she is shucking corn for dinner. She has on a sundress and is barefoot. In front of her is a large pot, and as she shucks she takes the freshly cleaned cobs and places them in it. For some reason this moves Betsy, and she can't keep her eyes off the girl.

For the remainder of her life she will remember this simple moment, a pretty girl shucking corn, and she will never tell anyone about it. And she does not know why this moves her so—could it be because it was something she did as a child when her parents had summer cookouts? No, it's bigger than that, it's more what the girl represents, this idea of family, and for the first time she sees herself as someone who should carry a legacy to a new generation. And that night, when they return to their apartment, the two of them gilded from gin and tonics in the sun, it is she who initiates the lovemaking, first with passionate kissing in the living room and then when they move to the bedroom and undress each other. In the dim light she looks up at Arthur, and he smiles warmly at her and brushes her hair off her forehead before he lifts her shirt up and over her head. And when Arthur reaches for the condoms in the top drawer of the nightstand next to the bed, she stops him.

"Not tonight," she says.

"No?" he says, surprised.

"No," she says.

And when he is inside her, she presses her face into the pillow, and her mind empties until there is only the simple feel of him, his hands on her hips, the strength of him, of her, of both of them.

The thing she imagines, before having a baby, that she will dislike the most, breastfeeding, she falls in love with. Seeing it from a distance, other women sneaking into the coatroom and sliding up their shirts, holding a screaming baby like a football, there was a primalness to it she found entirely unappealing: women as cows. But now, with Ethan, once she gets over the initial soreness and they figure it out together, how to latch, the two of them a team, she finds herself looking forward to it, the tug, the release of milk into his eager mouth. It is almost sexual, this feeling—but of course that cheapens it. It is more complex and nuanced than sex, more as if a fifth chamber in her heart has suddenly revealed itself.

He is more beautiful than other babies, she thinks, not

one of those weird old men. He has perfect features, and when he is nursing, she stares down at his beatific face and she loves him more than she thought it possible to love any living thing. Most of all she loves that she can give him this, the milk. The fact that she has this ability innately is as close as she has come to believing in God.

Later she will look back on this as the time in her life she was happiest. Ethan grows like a tree. Motherhood suits her. Arthur is a rising star in the classroom and even more so in the school at large. They have found their place fully in the world, and when that happens, you cannot help but feel it. It is as if their lives were locks that needed to be calibrated. Suddenly everything fits.

Soon Ethan is walking, banging into everything, muttering his first words. He is verbal early, and this pleases Arthur to no end, and when Arthur tells her excitedly, "I think he's smart. He looks smart, doesn't he? I mean, look at him."

"He'll be smart enough," Elizabeth says.

"No, I mean, he's got a gift. Look how quickly he's learning. He's so curious. He's like a scientist."

"All children are scientists," she tells Arthur.

And as Ethan grows, each year passing more quickly than the last, this is the only time there is any acrimony between the two of them. It is a question of expectations. She wants to build a shield around Ethan and protect him from his father's desires. Arthur sees his son's life with such narrative precision. He will become tall and handsome, a star athlete and accomplished student (in his field of choice, of course, as long as it is something traditional), and then Yale awaits after Lancaster, and then the return to Lancaster to take his rightful place in the classroom and wait his turn to move into the big white Colonial.

Maybe, Elizabeth thinks, she should have considered all this before she married Arthur. After all, it was pretty clear what came with Arthur, this explicit sense of primogeniture, but wasn't it also what she loved about him? That she could wear this old school like a blanket? Grow old inside its woolly warmth?

It is only through Ethan's eyes that it gives her pause. Ethan's eyes—brown as a doe's, heavy-lidded—do not have her husband's sharpness. Even in childhood pictures she has seen of Arthur there is a beady-eyed awareness in his brown eyes. But Ethan is an innocent, she thinks, surprised by anything other than straightforward benevolence. As for all children, the world is created for him every day anew, but unlike other children, he does seem open to this idea's being shattered, even when cruelty intrudes and does it for him.

Once, when he is four, at a July 4 faculty party, they set up a bike race for the kids. It is in front of the girls' dorms, and the kids race in groups by age. Ethan has his bike with the training wheels, and to the back of it he has attached, all on his own, a winter's plastic sled, and in it is his stuffed rabbit, Bun, which he carries everywhere with him under his arm. When the four-year-olds get their turn, Elizabeth approaches Ethan to help him, but he says, "Mama, I want to do it myself."

And he does. Down the road he goes with the other kids, pedaling his little heart out, the sled dragging noisily on the pavement. But when he gets close to the finish line, an older kid, maybe twelve and large for his age, steps in front of Ethan and impedes his progress. Elizabeth sees this blurrily, and she glances around for Arthur, but he has his back to the race, chatting with some of the men. Right then the larger boy throws Ethan off his bike and onto the ground.

Elizabeth bounds toward them, and Ethan is crying like mad, and the bigger boy is standing over him saying, "You can't have anything attached to your bike," like this is a race with rules.

It takes everything for Elizabeth to refrain from striking this boy who has pushed her son off his bike. Some big dumb kid standing in front of her shirtless, with downcast eyes, and she wants to run a knife through him.

She says to him, "Jesus, what's wrong with you? He's only four."

Ethan is wailing. "Mama, Mama, why did that boy do that?"

And the truth is Elizabeth has no idea. It is no big deal, a bully. There are bullies everywhere. But in that moment, she wants to tuck Ethan back in her womb, where he will always be warm and no one will try to hurt him again.

Arthur's father announces his resignation on a Friday in the spring. Elizabeth hears about it as a buzz that hums through the library.

"Did you hear about Mr. Winthrop? He is finished at the end of the year."

Elizabeth waits until before dinner, when they are in their dorm apartment, readying themselves to make their way as a family for their nightly trek to the dining hall, before she asks Arthur about it. Six-year-old Ethan is in his room playing with a model airplane. She can see him if she turns her head, carrying the small model over his head, making whooshing sounds.

Elizabeth says, "I heard today that your father has decided to retire."

"Yes," Arthur says, taking a pull on a glass of wine and then putting it down on the bureau, not turning around to face her. He is straightening his tie in the mirror.

"Did you know about this?"

"Not the exact timing," he says.

"What happens now?"

"There will be a search, of course."

"Are you a candidate?"

He turns toward her now and gives her a quick smile, then back to the mirror and his Windsor knot. "They will want to talk to me, I am sure."

"They will want to? What aren't you telling me, Arthur?"

He finishes with his tie and spins around and smiles. "Betsy," he says. "There is nothing to tell right now."

She looks toward the room where their son is now spinning in circles, dipping the plane in his right hand up and down above his bed. "Bullshit," she says a little loudly.

"Okay," he says. "Look. I can't have this around the school."

She might fall apart. "What do you know?"

He looks toward the window and then, gratuitously, toward the door, like some student might barge in and reveal their secret. "Okay," he says. "It's mine to lose. I think you are looking at the next head of school."

A huge grin sweeps across her face. "Holy crap, Arthur! I don't know what to say. This is unbelievable."

He likes this, her obvious happiness. He runs a hand through his hair. "Well, nothing is done now but . . ."

"What does this mean?"

He laughs. "No more living in a dorm, for one."

"Oh, that will be nice."

"Yes," he says. "Won't it? A fireplace? A big house? Are you ready?"

"I'm going to explode."

"You can't say anything."

She shook her head. "Who am I going to tell?"

"I know you won't."

"This is so amazing."

"And I didn't even tell you about the salary."

"Tell me," she says. "Tell me."

"Put it this way: Maybe we can get a place at the beach."

Elizabeth jumps to him then, jumps the few steps that stood between them, and he takes her in his arms. He gives her a stiffish hug, but it doesn't matter to her. Nothing can get in the way of her happiness. Who wants this more, she or he? Before she can decide, Ethan is there.

"Wash your hands," she says to Ethan. "We need to leave for dinner."

Walking across the expanse of lawn to the dining hall

and then, in the hall itself, sitting at their normal faculty table, she can hardly focus. She looks over to where her in-laws hold court at the most prestigious table at the far end, overlooking the entire room. She imagines sitting there. On the way back to the dorm, they pass the head-master's house. She has been by it thousands of times, in-side it hundreds of times, but this time is different, and while the three of them walk past, she stares into the lit windows and in her mind she is moving through that great house, sitting in front of the large fireplace with the logs replenished daily by the maintenance staff, hosting parties in the high-ceilinged rooms. She looks over at her husband and for the first time in a while she sees him as she imagines others see him—this man who aspires to greatness, a man elevated above his peers, and she is proud of him.

The following Monday, Arthur spends the entire after-noon with the trustees. She knows what they are discuss-ing. She has no idea how it is going. By four she leaves the library and gets home, but there is still no word from him. She walks over to Fuller Hall, where one of the dorm parents is a woman her age who teaches math. Her name is Karen, and if she is surprised to see Elizabeth she doesn't say anything.

"Betsy," she says. "Come in."

"You have a cigarette?"

"I didn't know you smoked."

"Today I do."

The students are all at athletics, and the two women smoke like teenagers. They open one of the apartment windows that looks out toward the river and they stick their heads out and smoke quickly and frantically, listening for voices coming around the corner of the dorms.

Karen says, "Everything okay?"

Elizabeth blurts it out. "Arthur might be the next headmaster."

"Really?"

"Yes. For real. We may know today."

Karen looks over at her. Their faces are inches away. "Well, that's wonderful," she says, though Elizabeth is not sure she means it. Something in the way she says it, the slightest hint of an edge. She knows many of the other faculty members don't love Arthur. They admire him, sure, but there is always the sense that he hasn't had to work as hard for his.

"No one is supposed to know," Elizabeth says.

"I won't tell anyone," says Karen.

"You're a good friend."

"Oh, we're not friends."

Elizabeth turns to Karen, and the hurt, or perhaps the surprise, must show on her face. They are close enough to kiss. Karen says, "Oh, shit. I can't believe I just said that."

"It's okay."

"Really. I'm sorry, Betsy. That was stupid."

"Seriously, it's okay."

"Fuck," Karen says. "That was unartful. What I meant to say—oh, shit. I don't know. I guess that you have always been aloof. Somewhat, you know? I mean, not in a bad way. Just that you keep to yourself. I should just shut up."

Elizabeth takes a final drag on her cigarette. She looks over at Karen and then out to the river. "No," she says, "you are right about me."

"I didn't mean anything."

"I know you didn't."

"Really?"

"Yes."

Karen throws her cigarette stub out into the yard. Someone will think it belonged, illegally, to a student. It flips twice in the air before settling on the hard grass. "I still feel like a heel."

"Don't."

"Okay."

Returning to her apartment, she can tell from the moment Arthur looks at her—there is no hiding it—that he will be named headmaster. He makes a token play at fooling her, but even he knows it is no good. Instead he stands there with a shit-eating grin on his face and he just shrugs.

"It's done," he says.

Later, before they go to the dining hall for dinner, she takes a walk along the river. This is in April. The river has receded from its heights of a month ago, when it over-flowed its banks tumescent from snowmelt. It is one of the first warm days of spring, and from the lacrosse fields behind her she can hear the cries of girls running up and down. She follows the river from where it runs narrow and flush to the banks to where it widens and flattens before heading into New Hampshire.

Here there is the semblance of a beach, a sandy lip where the water ends and before the bank begins. Along it lie ribbons of detritus, branches and leaves and who knows what else the runoff has left there. Her father had a name for this, these ribbons, and for a moment she struggles to remember what he called them. Oh, yes, she thinks, the skins of winter. She always loved that term. The skins of winter. The winter sheds it skin every spring, her father explained. Just as we do at certain times in our lives. She thinks about this: people as snakes. She shed her skin when she first came to Lancaster. The day she became Betsy. And then again when she married, and then, of course, Ethan. Now, about to move into the big white house, she figures she is about to do it again.

She tries, sometimes, sitting up in Ethan's room and staring out the back during this, the longest of winters, to remember this old house with fresh eyes, as it was to her the summer they moved in. She tries to remember how much happiness a physical space could once give her. Those evenings when they first moved in, when Ethan had been tucked in and Arthur was up sipping his scotch in his office and looking over his papers, when she would just wander through it, discovering something new each time. A big house is full of surprises, she thought, and suddenly there would a charming stretch of wainscoting that had somehow escaped her gaze before, or her eyes would settle on one of the crooked diagonal Vermont vernacular windows that all these old houses seemed to have, a way of addressing the eaves, and she would stop and marvel at it.

But often those memories are hard to summon, so she goes for the easier ones—that first Christmas when they cut down the tree themselves, hauled it in front of the fireplace, only to discover that it was still three feet too tall. By the time they sawed it down to size, it was a square tree, and for years this was a great family joke, the year of the square tree. But then it didn't matter, for they had the annual Christmas party for all the faculty and staff, and she loved nothing more than seeing her house full of gay, flushed faces, the bounty of food filling the great dining room table, the fires roaring in the fireplaces, and the children running underfoot. Most of all she loved that this was her house, Arthur's, yes, but hers, too, the first lady of Lancaster, though no one used that term. Maybe Karen had been right: She was aloof. But now, at least, she had good reason to be. They were deeply part of this place, at the heart of it, really, but also, because of their station, they could be reserved. Should be reserved, Arthur would argue. "They don't all have to love us," Arthur said, "but they will respect us. Especially if we keep a proper remove."

She remembers, too, from that first Christmas, the look in her parents' eyes when they first toured the house, her father sitting in front of the fireplace with a beer and watching Ethan scramble on the ground tearing open presents. Her mother taking in the large kitchen built for catering, the views of the fields out back. She loved that her whole family could stay with them, wake up in the morning to the smell of freshly brewed coffee, that she could sit like an equal until late at night with her own parents, sipping wine in the warm glow of the living room with its high ceilings and its soft light.

There was a sense then that she had arrived. For this was all she wanted, wasn't it? This house, this school, this accomplished husband, this son of hers with handsome long lashes and perfect features. There was nothing for her to worry about other than what time she needed to be at the library. A perfectly scripted life, in other words, with regimented days and seasons defined as much by the rhythms of school as by the weather. It was beautiful to be part of something bigger than she. Something that stretched both backward, to generations that came before, and forward, purposefully, to generations that had not yet arrived. Her life had both symmetry and meaning and sometimes Elizabeth thought that was all one could possibly ask for.

And at the center of it all is Ethan. Is it possible to love anything more than she loves her son? She remembers her mother telling her that the day she stopped being selfish was the day Elizabeth was born. She never fully understood what this meant until Ethan came along. There are times when she looks at him—out on the soccer fields as an eighth-grader, running independently and fast, strong-thighed and muscular for his age—when the feelings that swell in her heart are so great she doesn't know where to put them. She is proud of him; she fears for him; she adores him the way one adores a new lover, not the sexual part, of course, but the part where the rest of the world recedes and all of life is distilled into the most elemental of human relationships, where you would gladly trade your life so that the other person might live, and you would, as well, consent to die if they ceased to exist.

Ethan is a sweet boy, though not a perfect child by any stretch. There are the usual adolescent troubles. Though he is an athlete by the time he is a freshman at Lancaster, she suspects he is smoking. She takes to smelling his fingers when he comes in at night after study hall, which he spends, like the other faculty brats and day students, in the library. Now and again she suspects he has been drinking, too, perhaps out in the woods with some of the other kids, and once it is unmistakable, the beer thick on his breath, and Arthur grounds him for a week, nothing but study hall and meals, classes and sports. He does not take him to the Disciplinary Committee, though they discuss it briefly, and she is in agreement with him that because Ethan does not live in the dorms, it is different. They are like parents to a day student, so why would they turn him in? "It would only hurt his chances of Yale," Arthur says. Which is not to say that Arthur isn't hard on Ethan. He is. And this is where she and Arthur tend to differ.

Perhaps, she imagines, it is a question of expectations. The deep love for Ethan she feels translates for her into wanting to shield him from everything. He is an okay student, nothing exceptional, and in truth he struggles with math and science, which she thinks is fine, since she and Arthur were both English majors. But Arthur, whose own father drove him hard, wants nothing less than for Ethan to be at or near the top of his class, which for Lancaster is saying something. He wants him to excel on the field as well, and while Ethan is a decent athlete, he doesn't start at soccer, and in lacrosse he doesn't even play varsity. He is a normal boy, good-looking and sensitive, attuned to others, with high emotional intelligence, she tells Arthur. He is well liked, and isn't that something?

"It'd be nice if he just had some high regular intelligence," Arthur says dismissively.

His junior year, a Saturday night. She is upstairs in bed reading. This is in the winter. Outside her frosted windows a soft snow falls in the light from the back porch of the house. Arthur is in his office doing who knows what. Certainly sipping scotch. He drinks lots of scotch now. Downstairs she hears the door open and then the sound of something crashing. She sits up in bed and she hears Arthur's footfalls on the staircase. Then she hears words, loud words, and she is out of bed in a flash, at the top of the staircase in her nightgown, and she sees her son and her husband grappling down in the front foyer. An antique lamp is broken on the ground in front of an end table.

"Hey," Elizabeth shouts. "Hey."

They both stop. She bounds down the stairs. They freeze and look up at her expectantly, as if she is about to do something. But as she gets closer, she sees in her son's eyes a blankness she has not seen before. Ethan is as tall as Arthur, and stouter, and their arms are on each other, like they are holding each other up. She does not quite understand what she is seeing until Arthur says, "He's really drunk."

Ethan looks down at her. His head lolls to one side. "Fuck you," he says. "Fuck both of you."

Arthur doesn't hesitate. He smashes Ethan across the face with his open palm and while she screams no, Ethan falls backward onto the hardwood floor.

Her heart rises in her chest, but he is fine, of course he is fine, it is a just a hard slap, but when he tries to get up, he stumbles and crashes into the wall.

He sleeps it off. And they don't talk about it again, other than an awkward parent-and-child conversation in the living room, when they tell him he is grounded for two weeks. This is the next morning. He is hungover and contrite. Though now and again, when he looks over at his father, Elizabeth can see a hatred in his eyes that she has not seen before. It was a slap, nothing more, really, and she can justify it the same way Arthur does. He deserved it, didn't he? He was belligerent and shitfaced and all that. Did Arthur really have a choice but to hit their son?

But at the same time, she knows something has been altered between the two of them. Or perhaps, she decides, it was there all along, a gulf just waiting to be explored by precisely this kind of incident.

At any rate, what is clear is that Ethan is not one who can drink. Some can hold it, and others cannot. What she saw in her son justifiably scared her. He was not there—no one was there. Just the brittle mask that, when lifted, showed only rage and anger. We all have it, she thinks, just some of us are better than others at burying it. It is a useful lesson to know that this is one thing her son does not excel at.

It is the second plane that does it. The first one is explainable, hearing it on the radio, an accident perhaps, maybe a small private plane, it is hard to know, in the confusion. But something in her gut tells her it is more than that—or was that later, with the benefit of hindsight?

But back at home, sitting on the couch with Ethan (Arthur still at the office), they watch the second plane go through the tower, and she no longer knows what she is looking at. She is grateful for Vermont. Nothing happens in Vermont. If this is the end of something, Vermont will be the last to feel it.

What she remembers from that day is the deep fear of the ineffable. The reports coming in on television of planes crashing everywhere. The Pentagon. Somewhere in Pennsylvania. It reminds her of the reports she read about when *War of the Worlds* was on the radio, and how people thought it was real. Here—the television cannot lie; there are the planes, there are the great plumes of smoke rising up over the city—there is no question it is real, but what are they looking at?

Soon Arthur is home, but he only adds to the alarm by saying that he heard that this is just the beginning. She shrieks in horror when the first tower collapses. She cries when the second tower collapses. Next to her on the couch, her son stares stoically at the television.

The worst part of this day for her, however, is before the towers collapse, when the television shows shadowy figures falling like stones down the sides of the building. The horror for her is unimaginable: people who know they are going to die and then choose the manner of their death. A world where falling from one of the tallest buildings possible is more desirable than being sucked into the fire behind you. She tries to imagine that choice for herself, but she cannot.

And then, a month later, it is Ethan's birthday—a big one; he is eighteen—and they are out at the only okay restaurant in town, a place that, oddly, serves only pasta. It is just the three of them. They are halfway through their smoked chicken with pesto when Ethan looks up at the two of them and says matter-of-factly, "I'm not going to Yale."

Elizabeth looks at Arthur. He swallows and then says, "No? There is someplace you like better."

"I'm joining the army," Ethan says.

Arthur snorts. "Don't be ridiculous."

Ethan shrugs and looks back to his pasta. Elizabeth shudders visibly and stares over at Arthur. This has to be a joke. This is something she and Arthur easily agree on. Not that they aren't patriots in their own way, and not that they don't love their country, etc., etc., but there are the usual caveats, and one thing they both know is that the army is not something their son would get involved in.

Ethan doesn't say anything. Arthur stares at him. "You are serious, aren't you?"

Ethan looks up again, for just a moment, then back to his plate. "It's what I want to do."

"Oh, don't be self-indulgent," Arthur says.

"Wouldn't Yale be more self-indulgent, Dad?" Ethan says.

"Listen," Arthur says, and Elizabeth can see he is deliberately restraining himself, though a flush has come over the back of his neck and there is a vein rising up on his forehead. "Look at me." Ethan looks up. "If this army thing is something you really want to do, then for

God's sake go to college first. Go in as an officer. Be a leader of men. The army will still be there four years from now."

This is precisely what Elizabeth would have said had she been able to say anything at all. This is her failure as a mother, she thinks: She is incapable of regulating the two men in her life.

Ethan says, "It's done."

"What do you mean 'it's done'?" Arthur says.

"I signed the papers today."

"Oh, Ethan," Elizabeth says, and she starts to cry. She does not want to be crying in this restaurant—there are other students, faculty—and it suddenly occurs to her that her son possesses the adult cruelty of a husband who tells his wife he wants a divorce in a crowded restaurant knowing she will not want a scene. There is a protocol the well bred always fall back on, even in the most trying of circumstances.

"Then unsign them," Arthur says.

"It doesn't work like that."

"You stupid boy. What do you want? To be a hero?"

"No," Ethan says. "Nothing like that."

"Then why?"

"I don't know," her son says. "It's just what I wanted to do, okay? I didn't expect you to like it."

"Honey," Elizabeth says softly, "we love you, you

know that. We just want the best for you. Your father and I—"

"Oh, shut it, Betsy," Arthur says. "You stupid shit, Ethan. You know that. You've been given every gift and you throw it away. How can you be this dumb? Huh? My son? How can you be this fucking stupid?"

Ethan stands up then. Elizabeth realizes that, near them, the restaurant has gone still. She glances around—eyes averted at other tables; people pretend they are not listening, though you can suddenly hear a pin drop. Ethan stands up, and he towers over the two of them, this son, this person they made, and he glares at Arthur, and Arthur says, "Sit down."

"I won't," Ethan says quietly, a steely whisper, and when Arthur goes to get up, Elizabeth, aware of the pregnancy of the moment, the need to get through it, pulls on his arm, and somehow, to her great relief, Arthur sinks into his chair.

Ethan turns and walks out. Six months later he will walk across the stage in the field house and accept his diploma from his father. They will shake hands, not like father and son, but like any other prep school kid fulfilling the time-honored Lancaster tradition of handing the headmaster marbles so as to see how he disposes of them. (Arthur is prepared, of course, with a bowl behind him on a table, having handed marbles to his own father a generation before.) Like his male classmates, Ethan is handsome and boyish with floppy hair.

And by September, when his friends are moving into dorm rooms at Yale and Middlebury and Dartmouth, he will be in Iraq.

S he lost Ethan and she thinks she might be losing Arthur. He sits up in his study and drinks all the time. He says he is working. Once, after he retires to his room—he has begun sleeping in the guest room—she walks into his office, and on his desk is one of the yellow legal pads he is always using to take notes for work. He has been writing on it, but instead of the usual notes about strategic planning or prospective donors or the other things that make up his work life, he has doodled all over the page like a high school student would. There are some immature sketches—one that looks like a penis; another a drawing of, of all things, a thumb. But the rest of the page is her name, scribbled all different ways, a hundred or so *Betsys*, and now and again, in the corners mainly, it reads, "Betsy and Arthur," like what a fourteen-year-old boy might write if he thought no one was looking. Something that should be carved into the bark of a tree.

And then there is the talking to himself. Arthur has always mumbled to himself. He has always had this disconcerting habit, especially when he is preparing for public remarks, of walking around practicing out loud. Times when she would walk in the kitchen and catch him saying, "My dear students," and then seeing her and stopping. "Was I saying that out loud?" he would ask.

"Yes," she would say.

"I need to quit that," he'd say.

She'd smile. "Yes, you do."

But after the funeral it becomes more common, and not tied to public speaking. He mutters around the house, and from her perch in the library, for the first time, she hears others comment on it. The headmaster is talking to himself, they say. And she is embarrassed for him, for the two of them, and she doesn't know what to say to him or to others. It is no longer just the charming quirk of another Lancaster academic, the old man in his tweed and his school tie. It contains the husk of madness.

One evening, with the snow falling outside the windows, she cannot stand it anymore. She goes to him in his office, and there he is, dropping the legal pad and his endless and mindless doodles and pretending to absentmindedly look at his e-mail on the laptop in front of him. She loathes him and loves him at the same time. How can it be both? Maybe it is because he has decided to fall away just when she needs him the most. Things like this can go one of two directions, she thinks, and he has chosen to leave. He is a coward.

"Arthur," she says. "You cannot pretend."

"Elizabeth," he says. "What is it?"

"You know what it is."

"Is this about Ethan?"

She goes at him then. "Goddamn it, Arthur, will you wake up? Will you?"

"Come here," he says. "Just come here."

Somehow he coaxes her into his lap. He looks into her eyes, like he has always done. "There, there," he says.

"Wake up," she says.

"I know, I know."

"No, you don't," she says. "You can't pretend, Arthur. You know this, right?"

"Shush," he says, and it is patronizing, but he does have this way with her, and she looks into his brown eyes and she wants to believe whatever he says.

The craziest thing about grief, she decides in those moments when she is capable of such reflection, is how it numbs you. Nothing tastes good anymore. Nothing smells pretty. Sleep is elusive. She no longer dreams and she thinks this might be because the dreams come when she is awake. They are the only things that are vivid to Elizabeth, and not even the rare early spring day, when she feels the sun warm on her face, can take her out of this. Maybe if she had someone to talk to it would be better. But what can anyone possibly tell her that she cannot figure out on her own? Yes, others have grieved, but it is also so particular. She's not going to join some group so she can realize she is not alone. Nothing she feels surprises her, other than this: It does not get better. In fact, it gets worse. When they arrived at her door to let her know her son was dead, she thought, I can handle this; this isn't that bad. And then, in the days that followed, she thought, Look at me, I am handling it. I am strong and capable, as stout as a mother with a dead kid can be. But then it doesn't recede like the spring water. Instead it grows in intensity, like a virus that takes over her body, until it seems it is all she is. There is no more *her* any longer; there is just this thing that happened, the place in the world where her son used to be.

She spends a weekend up at her parents', and it is strange to be back in her childhood house, and at night she drinks tea with her mom and dad, and it is the same table where they once sat and talked for the first time about Lancaster School. They want her to talk, and she will not. So they sit in silence, and the windows rattle as they always have, with the wind coming across the highlands. Her parents sadden her. Her father's hands shake. Her mother doesn't hear well anymore, and makes a good show of pretending to listen to Elizabeth, to put together what it is she is saying, but Elizabeth knows that her own words come out of her mouth and just hang in the air before disappearing.

She wants to tell them that there is nothing left that matters to her. But she realizes that they still have her, and her sister, who has twins in middle school, and while her father still cannot hear Ethan's name without his eyes misting over, it is different for them. You get a second life as a parent when your children have children, your lifeblood flowing through a new generation, and this is something she will never know. She blames herself. They could have had a second child back then, and she did not want one. Maybe the ancient logic of multiple children is a guard against just this reality. The knowledge that if you lose one, there is always another to carry on for you. Some amount of love that will reflect back.

"You need to take care of yourself," her mother is telling her. "I am worried about you. You are so thin."

"I am fine," she says, though she knows that is not true.

"She's fine," her father says, still believing in her all these years later. "Leave her alone, will you? She's fine."

That night, she lies in her childhood bed and does not sleep. She watches the light of the full moon play off the pastureland and she lies there in the dark and in her mind she sees the entirety of the life her son did not have. She imagines the pretty girl he would have married. She imagines the children they would have had. She sees him, tall and strong and kind-eyed, holding a baby in his arms, bringing the baby over to her, looking down on its dewy eyes. She imagines the goodness he might have brought to their lives, holidays with his family that would have made the pain of getting old bearable. Summers on the Cape watching grandchildren dance in the breaking surf. It is the marrow of life, she thinks, family, and it has been taken away from her.

One spring morning she wakes to sunlight coming through the tops of the windows where the blinds don't reach. She gets a sense of blue sky. She rolls over and she does not know what time it is. Arthur is gone, of course, already left for the administration building. He might be mad but he is somehow still remarkably punctual. It is probably midmorning, and soon she will be expected at the library, though she is not thinking about that, not thinking about it at all.

She rises and considers her closet. All this waste, she thinks, looking over the array of dresses that have been worn only a few times, the piles of sweaters on the shelves, the shoes stacked neatly against the far wall. She was never much of a clotheshorse, but that is not what she is looking at. What she is looking at is the accrual of a life, things bought, things discarded, and somehow this is what has survived. All these sensible clothes.

She cannot be decisive, not today, and she turns away from them, and once again she is drawn to the blue sky sliding through the crack of sky. She goes to the hallway and for a moment she lingers at the top of the stairs—so grand, these stairs, swooping down and then around like something out of an old movie. The kind of stairs that women are carried up. She lingers there for a moment in her nightgown, and down below she can see the windows that line the front door, and the sunlight, the sunlight of spring, streams through them with a warmth that draws her.

Then down the stairs she goes, and instead of to the kitchen and to coffee, she goes to the door, opens it. The day is warm. The campus in front of her is silent. She watches a car make its way down the rural highway between their house and the other side, where the quad and the old part of Lancaster School are. Even though the day is warm, it is early spring and the grass on their front lawn still has patches of dirty snow in the corner, and the grass that is exposed is pressed down, brown and wet.

She can see between the buildings on the other side, and the walkways are all empty; no one is coming in and out of the doors. It must be second or third period, and everyone is in class. This brings a smile to her face for some reason, the clear regimentation, students and faculty moving with the synchronicity of swallows.

She steps onto the lawn and she grins again, this time from the cold and squish of the soft lawn on her bare feet, surprisingly pleasant, and then the feel of the slightly crunchy snow at the edges as she begins to walk. She walks around the house and then makes her way down the slight slope to the flat of the soccer field, and soon she is halfway across it, walking with purpose now, the sun warm on her face, though the breeze on her legs and ruffling her nightgown still has some of winter's breath.

In front of her are the girls' dorms, the low-slung brick buildings where she lived as a student almost forty years ago, and where she lived as a dorm parent ten years after that. They, too, look deserted, since everyone is on the other side of the campus.

She comes off the raised soccer field and onto the cold asphalt of the access road that runs in front of the dorms. She crosses it and then between her old dorm, Fuller, with Jameson to her right. On the left corner she passes the room she lived in her junior year and instinctively she looks toward the window, and because the shade is drawn, the only thing she sees is her reflection staring back at her, her hair wild, her face haggard with age and a morning without a shower or makeup. She looks like a ghost, she thinks, which in some ways she is.

She emerges on the other side, and at first she cannot see the river. She can see only the broad swath of land on the other side, snow-speckled, leading to the trees standing like rows of sentinels in the distance.

But, coming forward, stepping in deeper snow, up to her ankles in the lee of the building, she sees it now, a hint of blue caught in the sun. She walks until she reaches its banks and looks down at a winter's worth of runoff. The river is high and fast and silty, swirling and swirling with quick-moving currents. She stares at them. They are violent and almost mesmerizing. As if an invisible hand were running sticks angrily across the surface of the water. Breaking the plane and then pulling up suddenly, the ripple disappearing as if it has run its course.

The wind coming off the fields in front of her blows directly at her and takes the thin cloth of her nightgown and presses it tightly against her skin. She raises her arms to her side and holds them out and then she closes her eyes.

Falling is the easy part, she tells herself. We think it's not, but it is. We are just taught not to do it. All you have to do is say yes. Say yes, Betsy, she says. Just say yes.

She goes up on her tippy toes. She leans forward. She

opens her eyes as gravity does its work, and the last thing she sees is the blue sky, and the brown of the fields, and the water rushing toward her. She closes her eyes as she tumbles underneath it, instinctively holding her breath for the smallest of moments before allowing the river to fill her, suspend her, take her and not let go.

AFTER

R ussell Hurley turns toward one of the men.
      He says, "Do you think I could have a few min-
utes alone with Mr. Winthrop?"

The man nods. The two of them get up and leave the
room. Russell sits down across from Arthur. He studies
his eyes for signs of sentience, but it is like looking in a
mirror. All he sees is reflection, and he wonders if it will
be possible for Arthur to be whole again or if he will live
the rest of his life in the shadows.

"Arthur," he says. "I don't expect you to understand
everything."

"You can't be who you say you are."

"That's one of the things that will take time."

"I want to go now."

Russell looks around the room. It's windowless and positively Soviet. He doesn't blame Arthur, and though Arthur's crime is small, small compared to what he believes it to be, given his fractured, broken mind, it is unlikely he will just be released to take off his clothes in the park again. Instead, Russell thinks, the decision is more around where he will go. The police certainly don't want him; they just want him to be somewhere else, off the streets and out of sight.

"I know," Russell says. "I think I can help."

Arthur's head lifts slowly, and he looks at Russell. His narrow eyes squint. His head appears to be heavy on his shoulders, as if it's hard to hold up.

"How?" he asks.

"I think I can get you out of here, but you can help yourself, too."

"I don't understand."

"Arthur, I'm going to be straight with you. They are going to put you in Bellevue. Do you know what that is?"

"Of course. It's a mental hospital. Why would they put me there?"

"Arthur, I know you don't believe this. But you are not well."

"I am fine."

"I know. You are fine. Problem is *they* don't know that."

"Someone call Dick Ives. He will straighten this out.

Lancaster's attorney is Willard Bass from Bass, Frank, and O'Connor."

"Arthur—you can't win this. I'm sorry. I can get you out of Bellevue. But you need to agree to go somewhere else."

"Where?"

"A place in Connecticut. It's a residential facility. Very different from Bellevue. If you go there and do well you'll be home in no time."

"A hospital?"

"Yes, but it's not Bellevue. It looks more like a—it looks more like a boarding school."

Arthur sinks in his chair. He begins to run his hands through his hair over and over. Russell says, "You don't need to decide today. They will let you sleep now. Would you like that?"

"Yes."

"Okay, Arthur. I'll be back tomorrow morning, okay?"

Arthur nods, and Russell stands to leave. Arthur says, "Russell? You are Russell?"

Russell turns around and looks at the slender figure in clothes too big disappearing into the metal chair. "Yes?"

"I'm sorry."

"For what?"

"For everything."

Russell nods. "Me, too," he says.

Riding the subway uptown, moving with the train as it shudders around the bends with the lights flickering, Russell thinks about the randomness of life. It was entirely arbitrary that he happened to hear the name Arthur Winthrop as he moved through the hallway of the D.A.'s office yesterday morning and decided to stop one of his younger colleagues, who told him the story of the headmaster in the park. It was hardly a serious crime and never would otherwise have come to his attention, if it hadn't been for the station of the person involved, which made for good office gossip. Even though Russell had been at Lancaster for only four months, for some reason all these years they had kept him on the mailing list, and every three months or so the glossy magazine showed up at his apartment, pictures of Arthur everywhere, and sometimes pictures of Betsy, so in this way he has watched the two of them grow older, like a celebrity couple you follow in the newspapers. And sometimes, looking at Betsy, he got pangs of remembrance, but then he would stop and chastise himself, how silly it was, and how long ago. It doesn't make any sense to mourn the loss of something that happened when you were a teenager, though there were other times when he thought in some ways everything that had happened since in his life traced back to that short time he had had on that campus.

But after he heard Arthur's name and asked what was being done, it took only a moment for him to decide to involve himself. He placed the call to the school, and after a long pause he was talking to Betsy, and on the phone, things changed for him. There she was, telling him things like an old friend—that they had lost their son, that Arthur had lost his mind, that she had tried to take her own life. She said they had a horrible row when she was in the hospital recovering from hypothermia—a student had found her crawling toward the dorm after she came out of the river. She blamed Arthur for their son's death and she knew it was unfair but she needed to say it and she did. After that, he disappeared. Until the call from the NYPD that he was in custody.

And so he found himself telling Betsy to have the

lawyers hold on, that he would take care of it, all of it. And he heard the relief in her voice and the trust coming across the decades and through the phone. "Come down here," he said. "It will be okay. I promise."

He exits the subway and on Amsterdam he stops at Planet Sushi and orders two sushi dinners and an extra order of the hamachi. This is one of those nights when he wishes he knew how to cook, wishes he had one good dish he could execute, even if it was pasta with clams or something like that. But since he divorced ten years ago and moved to the one-bedroom with its view of the Hudson, he turned his refrigerator off and took the door off of it and filled it with books. The stove, also unplugged, holds in its oven his important papers, his birth certificate and passport and so on, since he figures if there is ever a fire, this is the one place that will withstand it. And New York allows you those possibilities, he thinks, the ability not to have to do anything for yourself.

Out on the avenue the night is dark and cold, and the streets are full of people walking huddled and faceless against it. Coming down Ninety-second, he can see the river now beyond in the icy dark and, as he enters his unassuming apartment building, he has this sudden sinking feeling that she will no longer be upstairs.

He rides the elevator to the fourteenth floor, and Mrs.

Goldsmith, well into her eighties, is in the hallway, her groceries at her feet, her terrier looking up at him expectantly as she fumbles through her bag for her keys. Russell desperately doesn't want to talk with her, not tonight, but she sees him and breaks into a wide smile, and he says, "Let me give you a hand with those."

A moment later he has Mrs. Goldsmith safely in her apartment, her groceries on the kitchen table, and he opens the door to his own apartment and for a moment he thinks his fears are to be realized, as the kitchen is dark and in the small living room there is only the light from the reading lamp and there is no sign of her. But then he sees the bathroom door is closed, yellow light coming from underneath it. He goes to it and says, "Betsy?"

"Oh," the voice comes back to him, and he is relieved. "Just finishing in the tub. Be out in a minute."

Russell quickly hustles and turns on lights, cleans off the small dining room table in front of the best feature of his place, the large window that looks out over West End Avenue to the wide Hudson and the twinkling lights of New Jersey on the opposite shore. He considers candles—he knows he has them somewhere, in the kitchen perhaps—but that would be too much, he decides, deliberately romantic. That is not why she is here, though, from the moment he saw her yesterday, for the first time since they were in boarding school together so long ago, he has allowed himself the fantasy, and why not? He is single, and he suspects, from the few things she has said opaquely, that she has left Arthur for good. But more than that, standing in front of her for the first time in fortysomething years, he realized that she has aged, of course, as has he, but that the ineffable part of her beauty, the part he thought about all the time during that interminable six months after he left Lancaster and before he started as a freshman at Brandeis, had not changed one bit. Even with short gray hair and the furrowed lines of late middle age, he would have recognized her on the street. And, he thinks, she is even more beautiful now to him, if that is possible. She wears her sorrow like clothes, but with wisdom and loss and years of living come a different, particular beauty that no smooth-faced adolescent can possibly match.

When she comes out finally, flushed from the heat of the bath, and wearing a T-shirt and jeans, he smiles at her. The table by the window is set. It is hardly elegant, with the containers of sushi simply opened, but he does have small plates and wineglasses and an open bottle of rosé, more of a summer thing than winter, but he couldn't think what else made sense with the fish.

"Oh, lovely," she says.

"I hope you like sushi."

"I do," says Betsy.

And she sits down across from him, and when she does he looks her in the eye and he thinks how much time can steal from us, what a goddamn thief it is, that an entire lifetime could be lived since he last sat with her. They should be strangers but he does not feel that way. He is comfortable with her, and he has been alone so long he decided a few years ago that he might never be comfortable with someone again. But here he is, the great irony, sitting across from Betsy Pappas (for, in his mind, that is what he will call her), and the years have stripped away. He permits himself to imagine that maybe this is just another Wednesday at their city apartment. Their kids are out and about in the world, living splendid lives. They will small-talk about what each of them did that day, about the children, who might have called with some new bit of news. Perhaps a new boyfriend or girlfriend or something they can collectively worry about.

She jars him out of this. "How is Arthur?"

Russell shrugs. "He'll be okay."

"Really?"

"Yes. I think so."

"Are they going to keep him?"

"They don't want to. I proposed a solution."

"Oh?"

"Stamford Hills. A facility in Connecticut. He'll get the help he needs. But it won't be Bellevue. He may even like it there."

Betsy raises her glass. She leans it toward Russell's. "Thank you."

He tips his glass into hers. "He still needs to agree."

"He will, won't he?"

"I think so," says Russell.

They eat. Russell watches as she takes a piece of slender fish into her mouth, dipping it first into soy, and he follows. She is skillful with the chopsticks—smearing wasabi on the fish, and all of it is seamless, and for a few moments they eat in silence.

"This is wonderful," she says.

He shrugs. "I wish I could cook, but New York always has sushi."

She smiles, and in the smile he sees her younger self once again and suddenly he is insecure for all the years he has worked and lived. What does he have to show for it? This apartment? He doesn't even have a tiny spit of land. All he has is this apartment on the Upper West Side, a failed marriage, but at least there are children who think fondly of him. He has his job as an assistant district attorney, one of many. He will never be district attorney, for this is Manhattan, and he is not that person. Perhaps in a small town, where he came from, but he always had different aspirations, didn't he? Otherwise he would not have gone to Lancaster, which is not the place for the son of a plumber from Western Mass.

They eat. For a moment there is only the sound of chopsticks picking up shiny pieces of fish on rice, dipping them into soy sauce and wasabi and then lifting up to their mouths. He watches her. She enjoys eating, and though he has no right to do so, he loves her for this.

Finally, he says, "I have to ask you. I am sorry."

"Say it," she says.

He hesitates. He sips from his wine. "Okay," he says. "Shit, I don't know how to say it."

"Just say it. You can ask me anything."

He breathes deep. "It's none of my business."

"Go ahead."

"You tried to kill yourself."

"Yes."

"But you didn't."

"No."

"Why?"

She puts down her chopsticks. She looks out the window.

He says, "You don't have to say anything."

"No," she says, turning back to him. "I want to. This is important."

"Okay," he says.

"I couldn't."

"Okay."

"I mean: I couldn't. Something happened. I jumped, right? Jumped into the frozen water. I wanted to die, I did. I wanted it all to go away. I wasn't well. I really wanted it to go away. But then something happened."

"What?"

"I hit the water and I sank. It was so cold. Coldest thing I ever felt. And it was like—it was like hands pulling me down. It was so easy. Just go, Betsy, I thought. Let go. But then suddenly I didn't want to. It was like my body said, 'Fuck that. You need to live.' I remember looking up, and everything was hazy. I couldn't see anything. Next thing I was above the water gasping. I wanted air more than anything. And I swam. I didn't know I could swim. How silly is that? But I did. I swam. It was like someone else was swimming for me."

"You wanted to live."

She smiled. Played with a piece of salmon on her plate. Outside, a barge moved down the river, and he saw it from his peripheral vision, lit like a Christmas tree. "Yes, I guess that's true. Something wanted me to live."

"Something?"

"It was so cold, Russell. I can't remember what I was thinking. I just went for the bank as fast as I could. And when I climbed up it, I knew I wanted to live. I knew I needed to live. Maybe for Ethan, though I know that sounds hokey."

"It doesn't."

"You're kind."

"There's nothing I can say that will sound right."

"I always loved that about you."

"What?"

"Your honesty."

"I work for the district attorney."

"No, it's not that."

"What is it?"

"I don't know. Something about you. I don't know. You are only yourself."

"I know," he says.

She cocks her head. "Yes, you do. That is your beauty."

He laughs. "I didn't know I had beauty. I mean, look at me . . ."

"I like you," she says.

"You once loved me," he says wistfully and then immediately regrets giving this idea words. "I'm sorry," he says.

"That was another life," she says.

"Yes," he says.

"I didn't mean anything by that," she says.

"I know."

They sit in silence. He reflexively takes a piece of

dragon roll into his mouth, though he is not hungry. He eats because it gives him something to do with his big hands. It gives him something to do besides stare into her green eyes.

He says, "I have overstepped."

"No," she says.

"Arthur—are you?"

"We were done a long time ago," she says.

"Okay," he says.

"I want him to be well."

"He will."

"I hope so."

"Betsy?"

"Yes?"

"I don't want to be foolish."

"Stop."

"Okay."

"I mean I am not ready for anything, you know?"

"Yes," he says.

She smiles. "Sushi is good."

"Sushi is great."

"Yes, it's great."

He drops his head and cracks a smile. She is across the table from him. He looks out to the winter night. It has been forever since someone else shared this space with him. And he thinks about the nature of the world, that after all

these years she is here and he loves her as if they were sixteen again, but he cannot say this to her, and that is okay,
that is as it should be. He looks out to the winter night.
Far below them is the river, timeless and uncaring. It moves
to the sea as if they were not there at all.

ACKNOWLEDGMENTS

I began this novel in the neonatal intensive care unit at Dartmouth-Hitchcock Medical Center in the summer of 2009. Our second daughter, Jane, had just been born and born far too early. She weighed less than two pounds. Her lungs didn't work. But nevertheless she was a miracle, and while I was in the middle of the arduous work of starting a college, I spent every moment I could next to her bedside during the six months she lived. And what began as one novel eventually became a very different one, a novel of grief and one that I dedicate to her, for though she did not live long, she taught everyone who came into touch with her the true meaning of courage and fearlessness. She was a remarkable brown-eyed baby girl, and this book, the most honest thing I have ever written, is for her.

ACKNOWLEDGMENTS

This book is also for her mother, Tia, the true hero of that time of our lives. This book is also for my daughter Sarah, who just turned seven. She is a marvel.

It is also for the amazing nurses and doctors at Dartmouth-Hitchcock. I especially want to give a shout-out to the nurses: Someday, if there is any justice in this world, nurses will inherit the earth. I need to single out a few of you by name: Ali, Angela, Christy, Donna, and Eneroliza. You were like family to us, and I don't know if we will cross paths again, but each of you is an amazing woman who gives so much love and labor to what you do.

I want to thank my agent, Marly Rusoff, without whom this book would not have been possible. She sets the standard for representation that every agent should aspire to.

My gratitude extends to the great Thomas Dunne, who saw in this book everything I had ever hoped a publisher could see in my work. I can't thank you enough for your warm welcome and for bringing this novel to the world.

Likewise, I also want to thank my editor at Thomas Dunne Books, the talented Anne Brewer, whose insights made this book so much stronger. And thanks to Peter Wolverton, for his leadership and advocacy on behalf of my novel.

I also want to thank my early readers and hope I don't miss any of you: Maura Greene, David Greene, Carolyn

ACKNOWLEDGMENTS

Greene, Meghan Westbrook, Miciah Bay Gault, Dana Routhier, Ann Wood, Alfred Donovan, and Alex Lehmann.

I would be remiss in not thanking all of my colleagues, trustees, staff, and faculty at Vermont College of Fine Arts. Your belief in my leadership and your willingness to give me the space to be an artist as well as your president mean the world to me. We are building something special and lasting together, and I am forever grateful to each one of you.

Finally, I need to thank my amazing parents for all their support of me and my work and especially for sacrificing to send me to Suffield Academy as a teenager. As my brother, Richard, recently put it, "If you hadn't gotten into all that trouble in public school this book would be called *The Principal's Wife,* and who wants to read that?"

DISCUSSION QUESTIONS

DISCUSSION QUESTIONS

1. What did you think were the central themes of the book, and how did they resonate with you?
2. The novel explores the taboo subject of a teacher-student affair. What did you think of the author's handling of this?
3. "Maybe, I think, this is what love is." There are several varieties of love portrayed in the book: passionate affairs, marriage, and parental love. Discuss the depiction of love in all of its forms.
4. The river is described as "timeless and uncaring." Explore the symbolic resonance of water in the book and what it means to the characters.
5. How did your opinion of the headmaster and his wife change throughout the course of the novel? Did you

understand them more having encountered both points of view?

6. "Time is malleable. Memory fails. Memory changes." Discuss the representation of time and memory throughout the pages of the book.

7. What do you think the structure of the novel brought to your reading experience? Did the narrative switch surprise you?

8. Ethan's death has a profound effect on his parents' lives. Explore the theme of loss and grief in the book.

9. What did you think of the author's representation of the boarding-school culture at Lancaster? Has it altered any of the views you currently hold?

10. Were you satisfied with the ending of the novel? Which character did you sympathize with most, and why?